Rites of Assent

In the series

BORDER LINES: WORKS IN TRANSLATION

A project of the Creative Writing Program at Temple University
Lawrence Venuti, General Editor

Rites of Assent

TWO NOVELLAS

Abd al-Hakim Qasim

TRANSLATED WITH NOTES
BY PETER THEROUX

Introduction by Samia Mehrez

TEMPLE UNIVERSITY PRESS
PHILADELPHIA

Originally published as *Al-Mahdi* and *Turaf min khabar al-âkhira* by
Dâr al-Tanwîr
© 1984 by A. H. Qasim

Temple University Press, Philadelphia 19122
Translation and Notes © 1995 by Peter Theroux
All rights reserved
Published 1995

⊗ The paper used in this publication meets the
requirements of the American National Standard for
Information Sciences—Permanence of Paper for
Printed Library Materials, ANSI Z39.48–1984

Printed in the United States of America

Text design by Kate Nichols

Library of Congress Cataloging-in-Publication Data

Qāsim, ʿAbd al-Ḥakīm.
    [Maḥdī. English]
    Rites of assent : two novellas / Abd al-Hakim Qasim : translated
by Peter Theroux.
        p.   cm. — (Border lines)
    Introd. by Samia Mehrez.
    ISBN 1-56639-353-1 (cloth : alk. paper). — ISBN 1-56639-354-X
(pbk. : alk. paper)
    I. Theroux, Peter. II. Qāsim, ʿAbd al-Ḥakīm. Turaf min khabar
al-ākhirah. English. III. Title. IV. Series : Border lines
(Philadelphia, Pa.).
PJ7858.A76M3513   1995
892'.736—dc20   95–14849

CONTENTS

TRANSLATOR'S ACKNOWLEDGMENTS

Virtually all of the textual obscurities of this work (obscure to me, that is) were brilliantly clarified thanks to the patient assistance of UCLA Arabic scholar Michael Fishbein. Any remaining imperfections are wholly my own.

PETER THEROUX

INTRODUCTION

In 1966, *The Smell of It,* a short novel by Sonallah Ibrahim,[1] destined to become one of the landmarks of modern Arabic literature, was published in Egypt at the author's expense. Printed on its back cover was a manifesto-like statement, signed by a group of young writers seeking to clear a space for their experimental writings within a generally conformist literary field. The statement read as follows:

> *If this novel in your hands doesn't please you, it is not your fault, but rather that of the cultural and artistic atmosphere in which we live, which through the years has been con-*

[1] Sonallah Ibrahim, *The Smell of It,* trans. Denys Johnson-Davies (London: William Heinemann, 1971). It appeared in Arabic under the title *Tilka l-râ'iha* (Maktab Yulyu, 1966).

*trolled by traditional works and superficial, naïve phenom-
ena. To break with the prevailing artistic environment
which has solidified and hardened, we have chosen this
form of sincere and sometimes painful writing. . . .*

*These names, which you are not familiar with, will
present you with an art which also is unfamiliar. It is an art
concerned overwhelmingly with the attempt to express the
spirit of an age and the experience of a generation.[2]*

One of those "unfamiliar" names affixed to the bottom
of the statement was that of Abd al-Hakim Qasim, whose
short stories had already appeared in a few progressive literary journals. It was not long, however, before Qasim's name
became one of the most prominent in the Egyptian literary
field, with the publication in 1969 of his first novel, *The
Seven Days of Man,*[3] with which he reoriented the narrative
on the Egyptian village.

As the manifesto clearly indicates, Qasim belonged to a
generation of avant-garde writers, known to the Arab reader
as the sixties generation. This is the generation that started
off supporting the military coup led by General Gamal Abd
al-Nasir in 1952, gradually became disillusioned with the
increasingly authoritarian face of the "socialist" regime, and
finally ended up in its detention camps. Not only did this

---

[2] The whole text of the statement is quoted in Sonallah Ibrahim's introduction
to *Tilka l-râ'iha,* trans. Marilyn Booth in "The Experience of a Generation,"
Index on Censorship 16, 9 (1987): 19–22.

[3] Abd al-Hakim Qasim, *The Seven Days of Man,* trans. Joseph Norment Bell
(General Egyptian Book Organization, 1989). It appeared in Arabic under the
title *Ayyâm al-'insân al-sab'a* (Dâr al-kitâb al-'arabi, 1969).

generation bear the brunt of the confrontation with political power and the disheartening catastrophe of the Arab defeat by Israel in 1967, but it also had to struggle against the dominant aesthetic values of the time. Ironically, political confinement coupled with literary containment, if not total marginalization, led to a formidably innovative outburst that was to provide Egypt with most of its leading writers today, among whom Abd al-Hakim Qasim has left a unique imprint.

Like most of the members of this generation who redefined both socially and ideologically the profile of the Egyptian intellectual, Qasim was of a modest, rural background; for such as him, the new sociopolitical reality, brought about by the 1952 revolution, seemed to promise the possibility of a different future. He was born in 1935 in the small village of Mandara near the town of Tanta in the Egyptian Delta. Upon completing his high school education in Tanta, he moved to the capital during the mid-fifties where he took up small odd jobs.

For Qasim, as well as others, the move to Cairo was a mixed blessing. On the one hand, it meant intellectual growth and a chance for active political participation and the reshaping of the nation's history. On the other hand, it meant an alienating encounter with the urban "other," a nostalgia for a more familiar, rural self, total estrangement from the increasingly oppressive present, and ultimately mistrust of what the future might hold. Like many of his generation who shared the same dreams and disillusionments, Abd al-Hakim Qasim found himself arrested in 1960 for his involvement in underground leftist organizations. He spent four years in a detention camp, where he managed to produce several short stories and the first draft of his extraordinary novel *The Seven Days of Man*.[4] It was only in 1965, one year after his release, that he completed the law degree that he had started before his detention.

Whereas the sixties produced the militant intellectual in the Egyptian cultural field, the seventies dictated exile as the only possible means of survival for many of these former militants. In the face of various repressive measures taken by President Anwar al-Sadat against both liberals and leftists who had sided with the student movement on the eve of the 1973 October War, some of Egypt's most prominent writers and critics were forced to leave the country.[5] Even though Qasim initially went to West Germany in 1974 by official invitation to give a series of lectures at the Free University of Berlin, he ended up residing there, with his wife and two children, until 1985. The general political climate in Egypt together with his opposition to the Camp David Accords were responsible for this long period of exile, during which he worked as a night guard, among other modest jobs, and

[4] Maria Stagh, *The Limits of Freedom of Speech: Prose Literature and Prose Writers in Egypt under Nasser and Sadat* (Uppsala: Almqvist & Wiksell International, 1993), p. 348. According to interviews with Stagh conducted in December 1988 and November 1989, Qasim was arrested on December 24, 1960, and sentenced to five years imprisonment by a military court in 1962. He was detained in al-Wâhât al-khârija and released on May 14, 1964, some days after Nikita Khrushchev's arrival in Egypt on an official visit. See also Stagh's case study of Abd al-Hakim Qasim (pp. 303–7).

[5] For more detailed information on this period, see Stagh, *Limits of Freedom of Speech*, pp. 98–102.

started a doctoral dissertation (which remained unfinished) on the underground movement in Egypt during the sixties.

Qasim's encounter with the West, however, had very little to do with what was described in his predecessors' writings. Taha Hussein, Tawfiq al-Hakim, and Yahya Haqqi, for instance, all prominent intellectuals and towering figures of the Egyptian cultural elite, had been formed in and by the West. Given the historical and material circumstances surrounding his departure, Qasim's experience of the West foregrounded its other face: the marginalizing, inhuman, and racist one. Hence the problematic search for a national identity that had characterized much of the writings of Qasim's predecessors becomes rearticulated and redefined in his work. Rather than upholding the Western "other" as a model to be followed in constructing a modernist identity, Qasim's experience in exile led him back to his Islamic roots, perhaps as a logical reaction to the devalorization to which he was subject.

Unlike the triumphant homecomings of the previous generation, Qasim's return to Egypt was an ailing one, marked by various unexpected, extreme positions that bespoke his crisis of identity. Upon his return, he began to write a column for the weekly *al-Sha'b,* organ of the Labour Party (the populist-Islamicist opposition), in which he attacked former fellow militants and writers; then he sought to be elected to Parliament on the list of the leftist opposition party al-Tajammu' but was defeated. Finally, he fell prey to a stroke that left him bitter, weak, and mildly handicapped. He died on November 13, 1990, leaving behind him three novels; six collections of short stories, which included his novellas; one play; and an unfinished novel.

The successive appearance of Qasim's novels and collected stories during the eighties points not to periods of literary productivity but rather to his experience as a writer in exile: condemned in his own country, away from the public eye, and with few or no ties to local institutions or regional publishing outlets. The content, general structure, and style of Qasim's works further reflect his alienating stay in the West. The rupture with the homeland bred continuity in the narrative; with many texts centered on the young, maturing Abd al-Aziz, a Dedalus-like protagonist and haunting presence whose eye traces the various changes that beset his rural context, Qasim's work began to take on epic dimensions. The stories about Abd al-Aziz's village and people are interrelated and emphasize the centrality of rural society to Qasim's work, even during his years of exile. Narrated in a style that borrows its cadence and diction from classical and mystical Sufi texts, Qasim's work focuses, in many instances, on existential philosophical questions that reflect some of his own concerns while away from his homeland.

The Seven Days of Man, written early in Qasim's career, already maps out many of these characteristics. Its very title and structure echo the seven stages of Sufi rituals that, within the narrative, become successive chapters describing the intricate lives of the members of a Sufi order from the delta, who are preparing to go to the neighboring town of Tanta for their annual pilgrimage to the shrine of al-Sayyid al-Badawi, one of the foremost "saints" in Egypt's popular Islam.[6] Likewise, the language of the narrative imitates, to a great extent, the rhythm and lexicon of the mystical texts that the Sufi group in the novel gathers to read and recite. It is through the loving gaze of the child Abd al-Aziz, son of Haj Karim, the prominent leader of the group, that we come to know this little village in *The Seven Days of Man*. Even though the gaze becomes more critical as Abd al-Aziz leaves the village for the city, the love and nostalgia for this aging, disintegrating world of the Sufi brothers never completely disappear. This nostalgia reemerges and continues to haunt Abd al-Aziz in many more tales by Qasim that draw on the mystical tradition for style and rhythm.

Hence the return to a literary and cultural past actually predates Qasim's nine years of exile. Such a return to a mystical heritage almost coincides with the unbearable Arab defeat of the sixties, thus pointing, perhaps, to an already existing sense of exile and alienation even within the homeland: an internal exile that sent many writers of this generation in search of experimental narrative forms and a new literary language through which they could give vent to their rebellion and sense of loss.

Many critics have rightly noted that Qasim's narratives on the Egyptian village distinguish themselves from a long history of representations of rural society in Egypt. Like a handful of writers of his generation—Mohammad Mus-

---

[6] For a detailed account of *The Seven Days of Man,* see Roger Allen, *The Arabic Novel: An Historical and Critical Introduction* (Syracuse, N.Y.: Syracuse University Press, 1982), pp. 120–31.

tagab, Yahya Taher Abdallah, and Yusuf al-Qaʿid, to mention only a few—he was able to resurrect the Egyptian village from the all-too-familiar "romanticism" and "social realism" that characterized the earlier decades of the century. The small village was no longer a pretext for the literary text, where arguments on social injustice, backward conditions, and class differences could be inscribed. Rather, the village became the very raison d'être of the text, its main protagonist, brought to life through the representation of its social fabric, its internal image and language. Not a static space anymore, the village was depicted through its transformations, its relationship to the city, its confrontations and frustrations with power, and, finally, its dreams and its mythologies. In all of this, Qasim's work offers a unique example of the radical differences that separate his generation's representation of the village from those of previous generations. The sixties generation were not the alienated intellectuals of the first half of the century, torn between their indigenous reality and the Western model, harsh critics of their time and space; nor were they the bards of a social realism that dominated the literary field with the advent of the revolution. Qasim's generation had different social and ideological trajectories: having distanced themselves from the European model and the slogans of the dominant ideology, they focused their attention on *what* to represent and *how* to represent it.

Naturally, such a questioning attitude toward existing representations of the "real" opened up several avenues of experimentation and innovation that, throughout the sixties and even beyond, allowed for the emergence of the marginal within the literary text—socially, culturally, formally, and linguistically. The centrality of the members of the popular Sufi order to *The Seven Days of Man* is a case in point: rather than cast them in the dominant stereotype of the dervish (the Sufi disciple) as a half-crazed, asocial, and misfit individual, Qasim represents the "Brothers of the Path" as active members in the social and professional fabric of the village. Thus he restores to Sufism much of what it truly represented within the context of Egyptian society: an organized populist movement with its own historical institutions and rituals, more concerned with the inward, spiritual growth of the individual than the outward, social behavior that characterized the conformist and dogmatic face of Islam.

Al-Mahdi and *Good News from the Afterlife,* which constitute this volume, revisit and reshape many of Qasim's earlier concerns, whether they be ideological, cultural, or literary. Written in Berlin in 1977, *Al-Mahdi* is one of the most remarkable works by Qasim and is certainly a unique gem in contemporary Arabic literature. It was belatedly published in Beirut in 1984 with *Good News from the Afterlife* (also written in Berlin, in 1981), a less recognized but equally original text with regard to choice of subject matter, structure, and style.[7] Whereas *Al-Mahdi* exposes the dynamics of coercion and scapegoating in the world of the living, *Good News from the Afterlife* delves into the serenity and clear vision of the world of the dead. The disturbing questions that are raised by the

---

[7] Abd al-Hakim Qasim, *Al-Mahdi* and *Turaf min khabar al-âkhira* (Beirut: Dâr al-Tanwîr, 1984).

former text are, to some extent, confronted with in the latter, so that despite the evident differences between them, these two narratives may potentially be read as complements.

Through the profoundly moving story of the forced conversion to Islam of Awadallah, the umbrella maker, *Al-Mahdi* audaciously addresses the compromised position of a poor Coptic family caught between the rising popular, regimental power of the Muslim Brotherhood and the complicity and passivity of a more tolerant yet increasingly weak Sufi presence in rural Egypt. Even though the setting and context of *Al-Mahdi* are both local and culturally specific, this text succeeds in transcending its immediate boundaries through its sensitive reading of the universal dynamics of coercion, oppression, and hegemony. In the light of recent incidents in Egypt—the most shocking of which has been the 1994 stabbing of Naguib Mahfouz by a young Islamicist zealot—*Al-Mahdi* becomes a fearfully prophetic text that foresaw almost twenty years ago the dangers of excess.

Once more, it is through the critical yet distant and passive gaze of the young Abd al-Aziz that we meander through Qasim's mosaic-like text. The short juxtaposed narrative sequences that constitute *Al-Mahdi* allow for a vivid picture of life within a small hamlet that lies between the larger village of Mahallat al-Gayad and the neighboring town of Tanta in the delta. The initial scene introduces us to Ali Effendi, Abd al-Aziz's uncle and one of the Sufi brothers in the hamlet. Effendi speaks of the unifying, God-fearing impact that the teachings of the rising Muslim Brotherhood have had on the vying powerful families of Mahallat al-Gayad. The highly organized, dogmatic, and very public Islamic power of the Muslim Brotherhood is then contrasted with the more intimate, mystical, private gathering of the Sufi order to which Ali Effendi belongs. The second narrative sequence opens with Master Awadallah's exodus, with his Coptic family, from the town of Tanta in search of work. From then on, the sequences alternate in telling how Ali Effendi stumbles upon Awadallah, takes him in, like a good Muslim, and naively surrenders him to the Muslim Brothers, who through their zealous religious fervor and oppressive, disarming generosity coerce him into converting to Islam. On the market day that the Muslim Brothers set for publicly announcing and celebrating in the hamlet Awadallah's conversion, Ali Effendi begins to feel responsible for the fate of a delirious, dying Awadallah whom he sees paraded as the "saintly" al-Mahdi through the streets of the crazed village. The text closes with the death of Awadallah just before his conversion, with Fula, his wife, making the sign of the cross over his dead body.

Peter Theroux's wise decision to maintain the Arabic title *Al-Mahdi* untranslated calls for a brief explanation. The word in Arabic literally means "he who is guided by God and can therefore provide guidance, show the way, or lead" (to the true faith). Further, the figure of al-Mahdi has historical and legendary significance not only within Islamic culture but within the Judeo-Christian tradition as well. For some Shia Muslims, the Imam or spiritual leader al-Mahdi has not died but is hidden and is certain to return in order to deliver and restore the Muslim faith and nation. This belief in a second coming associates al-Mahdi with the messianic and the Christlike, as well as practices of scapegoating and crucifixions. The Arabic title consciously evokes all these associations, and the text itself proceeds to explode their irony, tension, and reversal through the Copt Awadallah al-Mahdi, who, during his last delirium before his public conversion, becomes Christ on his way to the crucifixion scene.

Whereas Al-Mahdi demonstrates a great economy of detail in depicting the intricacies of life in the village, *Good News from the Afterlife* meticulously renders the Islamic rituals that surround death, the descent into the grave, and the moment of judgment by the two angels Naker and Nakeer. Here again Qasim draws on formal Islamic teachings that animate the popular imagery as he dramatizes the judgment scene of the grave that supposedly awaits all human beings. However, rather than build on the popular, accusatory image of the angels, who are normally expected to list the sins of the deceased and their punishment, Qasim transforms Naker and Nakeer into sensitive ideologues and philosophers who debate questions of class, power, oppression, gender, and desire with the dead man.

The text begins with the grandson's journey through the alleys of the village to the beloved grandfather's house, where he rereads, with delight, the scrolls of their family tree, which traces back to the "saint" and founder of the village, Sidi Qutb. As the grandson contemplates the tree, he reflects on its mirror image underground and concludes that existence is twofold: half-apparent, half-hidden; half life, half death. The actual death of a neighbor in the village gives the grandson occasion to participate in the funerary rituals, which the narrator goes to great lengths to describe. It is under the effect of a sunstroke that the grandson makes his journey to the underworld, where he descends into the neighbor's grave and envisions, as it were, with exquisite detail a replay of the neighbor's life, his encounter with Naker and Nakeer, and, ultimately, his judgment. All of these sequences provide further occasion for reflections on life and death, on the meaning of deeds and the meaning of judgment. The narrative sequences of the text bear subtitles of the entire process, beginning with death and proceeding to the grave, the two angels, judgment, and, finally, resurrection, insisting once more on the twofold nature of existence and culminating in the grandson's delirious statement at the end: "We are the ones who carry more death than life in our bodies. Only we know the news of the afterlife. We are the ones who can give life to the mortal world."

In both *Al-Mahdi* and *Good News from the Afterlife,* Qasim adopts an omniscient point of view, as he often does in many of his other works. This all-knowing position, constructed in the predominance of narrative passages over dialogue (especially in *Good News*), joins with a marked tendency toward repetition and a style that oscillates between the classical and the mystical idiom to provide the texts with a chilling stillness, almost a sense of permanence. It is perhaps appropriate that this occurs in two texts written in exile by a man seeking to resurrect and recapture the homeland, in both life and death. Today, Peter Theroux's careful and elegant English translation recasts these two very special narratives for a

much wider audience whom Qasim did not have the chance
to know.

SAMIA MEHREZ
American University in Cairo

Al-Mahdi

Everyone was breathless whenever Uncle Ali Effendi spoke of Mahallat al-Gayad. It was a truly wondrous village: the streets bore names and the houses numbers. When the fiery heat intensified in the afternoon nap time, wagons drawn by government mules made the rounds, sprinkling the earth with water. Ali Effendi said that he had been the scribe of the village council in Mahallat al-Gayad and was on good terms with the mayor, and this mayor was a man with the rank and title of *Bey* and the head of a family of twenty-five thousand people, out of the town's forty thousand total inhabitants. This was the al-Mashriqi family. Yes. Their prestige resounded throughout the country, but the Bayumi family quarreled with them vainly over the mayoralty. The Bayumis were also a mean and quarrelsome family, and the war between them raged intermittently. Their hearts harbored spite and malice. Not one day passed without someone being killed, or livestock being poisoned, or a house burning down, or crops being uprooted. The breath of violence convulsed the town night and day; violence echoed in the neighboring areas, a violence that not even the government could quell. People still told the story of the Bank of Credit's granary: when the corn supply dwindled and the people were in a predicament, the whole town attacked the bank's barn and left not a trace of it behind. Even the Inspection Committee could not locate the spot where the barn had been.

Ali Effendi spoke, and the people listened and sighed deeply, *There is no power or strength save in God!* They pitied this Brother whose job had flung him far from the shelter of hope and the warmth of family, but he said that was in the past, the Muslim Brotherhood★ branch in the town had changed things and inclined people's hearts to Islam. It had turned hatred and rancor into solicitude for religion, and now the youths wore scout uniforms. Instead of shrieks,

★The Muslim Brotherhood is a religious-political organization that was founded in Ismailia, Egypt, in 1928 by Hasan al-Banna (1906–1949). It advocated a return to the Koran and core Islamic beliefs to promote a healthy, ethical, and modern Muslim society but became more extreme in the 1930s, rejecting "Westernization," secularism, and modernization. It founded a terrorist wing whose assassinations brought it into conflict with both the Egyptian monarchy and the revolutionaries who overthrew King Farouk I in 1952. The Brotherhood went underground from 1952 until the 1980s, when it reemerged as a political party seeking to transform Egypt into an Islamic state. Its traditional base of support has been the poor and working classes, with a small but significant membership in academia.

fights, and quarrels, cries of "God is great" and "Praise God" now resounded.

Abd al-Aziz, however, followed his words absentmindedly, uninvolved. His uncle had worked in this town for long years, and Abd al-Aziz had heard these same stories word for word as a child, then as a boy, and now as a young man. As a child, Abd al-Aziz had visited his uncle in Mahallat al-Gayad with his father, then as a boy all alone, and now he visited as a young man. He knew all the roads, surveyed all the houses, recognized all the people, and listened to these stories as a child, his heart nearly bursting with dazzlement. His uncle brought the stories to life so that a listener could practically see the action taking place. Abd al-Aziz was delighted when he first saw the houses, roads, and people; but these things had lost their warmth, staled and died, becoming dust. Now his uncle's voice softened, as he implored and pleaded:

"We are the Brothers of the Path. Our community is contrite by nature, and our motto is the beloved Prophet's saying, 'O God, let me live poor, die poor, and dwell among the throngs of the poor.'"

Ali said that after the evening prayers on Sunday and Thursday, the Brothers—God bless them!—met at the house of Sheikh Sayid al-Hasari. They assembled for the recitation of supplementary prayers for extra grace, the *Burdah* of al-Abasiri and the *Guide to Blessings* of al-Jazuli, and sought to read their fortunes in randomly chosen Koranic verses.★ Then they asked for God's mercy and, in closing, read prayers for the dead, engaging in informal conversations whose warmth stayed with them until they headed home to their beds, among their children. Here the relatives' hearts took comfort with regard to their brother transported by his job into remote exile, for protection among the Brothers of the Path is part of the safety of the family's quarters. And here, too, began a conversation dear to Abd al-Aziz's heart; he leaned over and paid closer attention, glowing whenever the subject of Sheikh Sayid the mat maker arose.

He had seen the sheikh here, and he had seen him in Mahallat al-Gayad. He was a quiet man with a soft voice—his speech was nearly a whisper—but his words lingered in the soul and smothered impatient thoughts with silence. His eyes were weak and his sight poor; he could hardly see. He was dry as a fallen branch. He was stooped from carrying bundles of reed mats and peddling them around the country; he offered them on his haunch, slung below his back, and his hands were tough as claws from plying the needle as he bound the mats. Abd al-Aziz entrusted him, whenever he saw him, with his hearing, heart, and mind.

Sheikh Sayid al-Hasari said that the people of Mahallat al-Gayad were extravagant, and this word led Abd al-Aziz's

★The *Burdah* is the "Ode to the Mantle" (Qasīdat al-Burdah) of the Egyptian poet al-Abasiri, or al-Busiri (d. 1295), a heavily mystical work beloved of Sufis. The *Guide to Blessings* (Dalā'il al-Khayrāt) was a similar prayer book by the Moroccan al-Jazūli (d. 1465), consisting of litanies and encomia of the prophet Muhammad. Both books identified Muhammad with the "Perfect Man," in a medieval Cult of the Prophet that still exists among Muslims inclined to the mystical and ascetic tenets of Sufism. Such works would be anathema to the literal-minded Muslim Brothers portrayed in *Al-Mahdi*.

heart into a profound silence. Of the two great families, Sheikh Sayid al-Hasari said:

"We are so preoccupied with our little affairs that they keep us from getting into great questions."

Abd al-Aziz did not fail to hear the pride of power in the ring of these words. Of the troubled events in Mahallat al-Gayad, Sheikh Sayid al-Hasari said:

"God has foreordained all deeds, and it is fitting for a slave that he choose what is least attractive, in order that there be peace, and that hearts may not be sleepless from fear."

Sheikh Sayid set out on his travels, and whenever he came or went, he did so very quietly, without ceremony.

Thus Ali Effendi's visit would be a test of their strong family ties, which proved themselves time after time. His visit was a comfort to Abd al-Aziz's heart. He loved this uncle, and he came every time with a bit of Sheikh Sayid's life story; it was a chance to forget himself for an hour and think.

$\mathcal{I}$t was midafternoon, the sun was gentle, and the air was fresh and pure. The canal water reflected the blue sky and cooled the lapping breezes. Master Awadallah Awadallah, the umbrella maker, carried his provisions on his shoulder, a small bag in one hand, and in the other, the hand of his son, Hantas. Behind him walked his wife, Fula, with a bundle on her head. In one hand she held a little basket, and in her other arm her daughter, Lawzah.

The breeze on Awadallah's brow cooled his sweat and lightened his weariness, or rather, turned it into a feeling of winey tipsiness. Walking through the stems and stalks filled him with delight and freed his soul from worry. Yes, Master Awadallah's heart had been heavy because of the situation with his landlady, Mrs. Gabuna. She was a kindly, animated lady who enjoyed the respect of the people and the honor of the neighborhood, but times had been very hard recently, and there was no money. For long months they paid her no rent for the room they occupied in the ground floor of her house. The lady made not a single complaint. Whenever she went down, she would knock on their door and stand off a little, timid.

"Master? Abu Hantas?"

He knew, when he went out every day carrying his provisions, making his rounds through the streets to repair umbrellas or make new ones and returning in the evening, that he would have barely enough in his pocket to keep his family alive. His wife, Umm Hantas, did her utmost and scrimped as much as she could, but there was never enough to pay the rent. He was filled with shame and grief and bowed his head, not daring to raise it to Mrs. Gabuna's face.

"God help us, ma'am."

Mrs. Gabuna said nothing but turned to ascend the stairs, then spoke.

"Don't be embarrassed by my coming to you. I only wanted to make sure you were all well."

He lingered, listening to her feet climb the steps until she was gone, then took refuge in his corner of the room but never closed his eyes.

This time, when he saw her standing timidly at the open door, he said:

"Mrs. Gabuna, I'm leaving. We will leave you these copper dishes to make up for our late rent."

Umm Hantas's face paled until it was white. She lifted her wide eyes to the master, and he looked down at her with a defeated, terrorized face. The children stopped chewing their bread, frightened. For a moment their eyes met.

"Get up, Umm Hantas," said Awadallah. "We're going to gather up our things and leave here."

The day was still young when they went out. Umm Hantas looked back for a last glimpse of the house in which she had long dwelled. She walked down the alley behind the master and spoke to some of the women sitting in their doorways.

"Good-bye."

Her neighbors asked her nothing. Perhaps they did not understand the change behind this exodus, perhaps it had not occurred to them, or perhaps it was too difficult for them to ask about.

"Good-bye," they said almost inaudibly.

Fula could feel the city receding behind her back and the littleness of their procession along this country road amid the vast fields, and she was seized by fear.

"Where are we going, master?" she whispered.

He did not look at her, but trained his eyes on the horizon. They kept walking, like two poor people under one blanket.

"I couldn't make a living in Tanta, Fula," Master Awadallah told her. "We'll go out into the country. We may find good fortune."

She was silent a little while, distracted, then spoke softly, as if to herself.

"Let's find a Christian village, Awadallah, with a church and a good priest."

A dream like the white wing of a boyish-faced angel brushed the side of his heart, and he sighed.

"Jesus will protect us, Fula."

Fula looked around her and swiftly made the sign of the cross, and Awadallah continued speaking in a low voice.

"The village chiefs and important men in the country don't wear those hats with tassels. Umbrellas give them prestige *and* shade."

Then he bared his foreheard to the breeze, and the bitter taste of exhaustion in his mouth mingled with the taste of his glistening tears as he murmured his prayers. ". . . Lead us not into temptation, but deliver us from evil . . ."

Ali Effendi closed his big notebook and pushed it aside after entering the mules' feed, then revised the expenditure vouchers from the original and three copies, working unhurriedly, singing softly to himself as his son Attiyah sat, his legs swinging down from the chair, laughingly watching his father.

"Abu Asakir!" called Ali Effendi.

A truly odd-looking man entered, diminutive and pain-fully thin, with a long face and narrow eyes but with a kind laugh. When he laughed, his eyes disappeared completely, but he could still see, at least. He could just barely find his way here and there in this village office; he was one of the perverse, sallow, emaciated sweepers, cart drivers, and stable hands, a leftover in this land of handsome people, mild-tempered and courteous among a people whose hostility and wickedness abounded, looking with their spies around Ali Effendi in the face of his constant rebuke.

"Abu Asakir, sir, come with me and I'll issue you the feed from the storehouse. And I swear to God, stop eating the nuts meant for the mules."

"That has not happened, Effendi."

"Don't hold God responsible for your faith, Abu Asakir. Eating the mules' nuts is a sin. Do you know why these mules are healthy and strong? Because they eat wisely, and they don't overeat. But you—if you get your meal at home, you'll bring in half a basket of bread, for sure. And the women have to spend their lives grinding grain and making dough and baking bread. And in the office, sir, you fill your room with the mules' nuts and spend all day cracking them."

"That has not happened, Effendi."

"And yet you're sallow, potbellied, you have indigestion. You don't heed the saying of the Prophet of God—'All disease is from the stomach, and zeal is the best medicine.' You have no zeal, just rancor, and your raids on the mules' feed."

Thus Ali walked through the courtyard of the office as

far as the storehouse, tall and slim, his fez on the back of his head exposing his thick, glossy black hair, chanting these words and stressing the end of each one, absentminded, his eyes not settling anywhere. He dispensed the feed to Abu Asakir, took his son's hand, and went to Niazi Effendi, the head of the office, who raised his head from his documents, startled, then stuttered awkwardly in apology for having interrupted. After some flattering smiles and a pat on the well-bred boy's head, Ali Effendi resumed his singsong words, relating what had happened that workday as Niazi Effendi signed vouchers.

"And so it went today, exalted sir, and so it ended, and so I seek your leave to go home."

"In God's keeping, Ali Effendi."

"Will you do us the honor of having lunch with us today?"

"I would love to, but my wife and the children are in Tanta."

"So we are out of luck. No fortune. No way around it. Good-bye, and give your family our best."

This rite ended the work of the day. Ali Effendi bid Abu Asakir a good afternoon and proceeded through the neighborhoods of Mahallat al-Gayad under the noonday sun, greeting people and asking them how they were. He bought dates and guavas and headed home, his arms loaded with purchases, to his wife, who silently rushed to him, her eyes examining his features, which were frankly feverish and exasperated. She took the groceries from him and he handed her his fez.

"The whole house smells of *mulukhiyah*," he said.★
"*Mulukhiyah* and rabbits?"

"We slaughtered the little black one. The old peasant man caught and skinned him."

Attiyah burst into tears.

"You killed my rabbit!" he sobbed.

"No, sweetheart," his mother said quickly. "Your white rabbit is still there—go in and see for yourself."

After the afternoon prayer, Ali Effendi went out, as was his daily custom, to the center of town, to the main street lined on both sides with willow trees. On this particular afternoon he found Master Awadallah Awadallah, his wife, Fula, and their children, Lawzah and Hantas, on the side of the road. When he came near them, he knew from their faces that they were Copts, and his supposition was confirmed by the crosses tattooed on their wrists. He did not greet them by saying *salaam aleikum*.

"Good day," he said instead.

"Good day to you," said Master Awadallah hastily, disconcerted.

Ali Effendi looked around and found a big rock; he sat down on it and held Attiyah to his chest, ready for a long, pleasant midafternoon conversation.

★*Mulukhiyah*, or "Jew's mallow" (*Corchorus olitorius*), is an Egyptian plant whose pounded leaves produce a soupy, dark green sauce, generally served with chicken or over rice.

*M*aster Awadallah, at the head of his little band, kept journeying along the farm road for a long, long time, as the people of the city came out of their vile confinement into the vastness of the country air, intoxicated by the open horizons. As he walked, he was not overtaken by fatigue until after some time, when he came upon the first village that appeared, he and his group sat down on its outskirts. He took out his things and was busily engaged in his craft while the two children played in the dirt. Fula was silent, immersed in anxieties, watching his untiring hands as they deployed his tools. A few customers squatted around Master Awadallah; this was a good omen, but country people were poor, and they were afraid of falling into the snares of city people. Master Awadallah smiled sadly, a smile of despair, and his wife watched him in silence. She saw him lower his price time after time, contenting himself with whatever he could earn. They ate the bread and salted cucumbers the peasants gave him and slept wherever evening overtook them.

"I am an umbrella maker," Awadallah said when the watchman came at night. "I go around villages trying to make a living."

He offered the guard a cigarette, and he sat down with Awadallah, gratefully smoking the cigarette and chatting for a while before going on alone. So it went, in village after village; slowly, slowly, fear crept into Master Awadallah's bones, and without a word it spread from him to his wife, Fula. The children's silence grew more profound, as did their questioning gazes at their parents. What next? Day followed day, and his living was sufficient. What next? The vastness of the horizon was terrifying. He looked around him, and from the depths of his heart he silently cried out, O Jesus Christ, Son of God . . .

As if Fula could hear his heart's prayer, which his lips did not whisper, she too stammered:

"Jesus, Son of God."

They resumed their journey until they saw Mahallat al-Gayad in the distance. Master Awadallah marveled at the lovely street, bent over, and sat down, resting his back against a tree. He took out his tools, spread them out, and began to apply himself to his craft, until the sun was about to set—not a single customer had shown up, but now Ali Effendi came upon him.

"So you are an umbrella maker, my man," said Ali Effendi.

"Yes, sir."

"There are no finer craftsmen than the Copts."

Master Awadallah smiled warily, and Fula gathered up her cloak around her.

"There are many Muslims in this trade, and they are all excellent," said Awadallah, adding, "There are lots of livings to be made."

"Yes, yes," Ali Effendi assured him. "And you, it seems, live in Tanta."

Awadallah could not fight the pounding of his heart; he was tired and hungry.

"We used to, but we were far behind in paying the rent, and our landlady—"

"What is her name?" Ali asked, interrupting him in his surprise.

"Mrs. Gabuna."

"God shame her!"

Awadallah was alarmed at the misunderstanding he had caused and said, "She—" but was interrupted by an agitated Ali Effendi.

"Throwing you into the street like that!" He sprang to his feet and announced gallantly, "Come with me, man, with your children, to my house, as an honored guest, until God gives us morning."

Awadallah and Fula exchanged looks of despair that penetrated into the soul of the other, and Awadallah lifted a beseeching face to Ali Effendi.

"By God, please excuse us. We do not want to be a burden to you."

But Ali Effendi's determination swept everything before it, and there was no resisting.

"Gather up your things, man, and get up. A man gets nothing in this world of ours unless he honors guests. Gather up your things and get up, and God shame that Gabuna!"

He turned to Fula, who was motionless and silent.

"And you, my lady, get up. All is still well with the world."

Then he took Attiyah and Lawzah each by one hand and began to walk with them. There was nothing Master Awadallah could do to stand in the way of Ali Effendi's will: he was tired and hungry, so he walked behind him carrying his bag. Ali Effendi in his splendid white robe strode leisurely ahead, greeting everyone he saw, laughing with them and

answering questions, until his triumphal procession ended at
his house. He pushed open the door, went inside with the
children, his two guests behind him, and called out.

"Children! Children!"

His wife came out to him, their perplexed-looking
daughters behind her.

"Good has honored us with guests," he smiled. "Good
people, thrown into the street by their landlady, named Gabuna, without pity."

His wife looked at the guests silently, then whispered,
"Welcome."

Time stopped for a moment, with all of them standing,
not knowing what to do, so Ali Effendi took the initiative to
speak and give his wife orders.

"You know that little room. Clean it up well, put in
fresh mats, and fix up a bed and pillows. Find a nice lamp,
some water, and a chamber pot for the children. Do I have
to list everything you need to do?"

"We'll do it," said his wife meekly.

"Prepare some supper for them in their room," Ali Effendi went on in his commanding tone. "They are very shy
people, and if they ate with us, they might be too embarrassed to eat much."

"Yes, sir," said his wife.

When the door of the room closed upon them,
Awadallah felt that he had fallen into a pit. His body was
hard with fear, and Fula was pale and bug-eyed. This was a
nightmare. How had one day delivered him to the next, and

the next, to arrive at this strange hour? How could he have been so stupid as to abuse Mrs. Gabuna? She was kind and honest and did nothing to hurt them.

"I wish we could get out of here," said Fula in a trembling voice.

"How?" whispered Awadallah.

"I'm hungry," Lawzah begged them.

Fula broke off some bread in a dish, poured *mulukhiyah* over it, and felt almost like vomiting at the greasiness of the food. Awadallah was frightened and said to her:

"We should eat something too. We have to eat something."

Abd al-Aziz knew Brother Talaat. He had seen him for the first time in class at Tanta High School; it may have been Talaat's first class at that school. The teacher was quarrelsome and severe. He asked a question of Talaat, who diffidently stood up to reply, tremendously tall and broad-shouldered. Nothing was easy for him. Perhaps because Talaat was so large and imposing, the teachers went into a rage and slapped him across the face. Abd al-Aziz was terrified and looked at Talaat's face and the red mark of the teacher's hand on his upper cheek. Abd al-Aziz imagined that the force of the blow had dented Talaat's face and made it perversely flat as he stood, his jaw slack and bug-eyed, but Abd al-Aziz later discovered that Talaat had been born that way, his head as flat as a round loaf of bread on his shoulders. He also discovered that Talaat was afflicted with a deviated septum and always

breathed through his mouth. Perhaps this changed the taste
of his saliva or dried out his throat; you always saw him
sucking moisture into his mouth audibly. His gums bled in-
cessantly, which made his smile nauseating, but he was a
good person and rather simple-minded. He looked curiously
at the expressions on the faces around him, anxious and
fawning. Abd al-Aziz had come to know him at Muslim
Brotherhood meetings and learned, to his delight, that he
was from Mahallat al-Gayad.

"Do you know Ali Effendi in the village council?" he
asked him.

"I know him," Talaat smiled. "Ask him about me. Ask
him if he knows Talaat Mashriqi."

"Are you from the Mashriqi family?" asked Abd al-Aziz.

He smiled that same smile and murmured his assent.
When Abd al-Aziz next met Uncle Ali Effendi and asked
him about Talaat Mashriqi, his uncle was surprised and
curled his lip scornfully.

"That's pretty blatant, trying to associate himself with
the Mashriqi family. His father took the name Mashriqi only
to ingratiate himself with that family. He is from the small,
starving Abu Habbah family. His father is a minor school-
teacher in the government school."

Abd al-Aziz was very surprised at this but said to himself
that there was nothing wrong with a person coming from a
poor, unimportant family; a man could make his own way,
and Brother Talaat was one of the most active young men in
the Brotherhood at school. Everyone had approved him as a
scholarship student, so the mission gave him a charitable sti-

pend after the previous recipient received his high school diploma and went on to the university. Talaat had a fat, pale brother at al-Azhar University who came from Cairo with a huge folder of papers, seeming tired and distracted. The Brotherhood of Tanta welcomed him with open arms. While he stood delivering a sermon, he fired them up with an eloquence that made them forget everything else; Talaat watched from a distance, smiling with pleasure. Abd al-Aziz never forgot to see Talaat on his visits to Mahallat al-Gayad, and even after they had both moved on to the university and Abd al-Aziz's relations with the Brotherhood slackened and then ended altogether, he asked about Talaat in Mahallat al-Gayad and saw that he was very active and that everyone was talking about him. He was all over town, night and day, doing the Brotherhood's work.

Abd al-Aziz later learned that Talaat, who always found time for people despite his many commitments, had met Ali Effendi, who was on his way back that night from an evening of prayer with the Sufi brotherhood at the home of Sheikh Sayid al-Hasari. "Peace upon you, Ali Effendi, and God's mercy" was Talaat's greeting to Uncle Ali Effendi.

"And upon you peace, Talaat, sir, and the mercy and blessings of God, and a very good evening to you."

"I wish you'd call me Brother, not sir—it's closer to the heart."

"You are our brother and our respected sir."

"God help me! Thank you! We'd love to see you sometime at our mission."

"The mission is in all our hearts, but our group devotes

its meetings to reading fortunes and reading the *Burdah* of al-Abasiri."

"God's scripture is more important and more beneficial."

"Every word in it is the breath of God, Brother Talaat."

"Even the hallucinations of dervishes?"

"They are the servants of the holy men of God, and the perfume of his Prophet!"

"It is the faithful that are the servants of God, it has nothing to do with kinship, and 'Arabs are no better than non-Arabs unless they are more pious,' as the Prophet said."

"I am of a family honored to have touched the thresholds brushed by the perfume of God's Prophet."

"That is paganism."

Ali Effendi answered him with a few lilting verses:

"*I pass by the country, the country of Layla,*
I kiss this wall and that.
It is not love of the country that stole my heart
But love of her who dwelled in it."

"Read the Koran, Ali Effendi."

Ali Effendi did not like this didactic manner.

"Talaat, sir, I fill my heart with love."

"You are never out of our thoughts, Ali Effendi," said Talaat, resuming his flattering tone.

"God and I respect you, Brother Talaat," said Ali Effendi indulgently.

"God love you."

"By the way," said Ali, "I wanted to mention a good man to you, a Christian umbrella maker. He used to live in Tanta, but his Christian landlady kicked him out—she just threw him into the street, leaving him and his children homeless. I found them in the street and took them to my house. I would like the mission to take an interest in him."

"Strange!"

"His little boy and girl were pale with hunger."

"Of course we are interested in him. We must act charitably toward non-Muslims and incline their hearts to Islam. I'll drop in on you at the council, and we'll see what we can do."

"We'll have a nice glass of juice together."

"Good, because I don't smoke, or drink tea or coffee."

*M*ashriqi Bey, the mayor of Mahallat al-Gayad, woke from his sleep at noon, his eyes swollen and his mood very bad. Fatimah bint Abu Asakir, the new maid, told him that his bath was ready. He put on his wooden bath clogs and clomped along the tiles on the second floor of his large residence, his thin white nightshirt showing clearly his nakedness underneath. He let the cold living room cool the breath of his warm body. He delightedly poured hot water over himself, then lathered his body with soap several times and rinsed himself again with warm water, thinking of the girl Fatimah bint Abu Asakir and of her beautiful, round breasts. She had worked for a rich family in Cairo, so was clean, not chapped and rough like a country maid, washed clean of all that country dust. He fondled his male parts with pleasure, delighted at the thought of how he would take each of her breasts in a plump handful. He would get her into his big brass bed, and they would cavort naked under the blanket. His wife, with all of her prayers and "Praise Gods," could be damned. She had kicked him out of her life to the upper floor for years and never came up to see him, leaving the maids to look after him.

When he was done, he laughed as he dried himself off and went out to the balcony, where his breakfast was waiting on the little table. He sat down and dunked a large, fresh morsel of bread into cream and honey and watched the girl Fatimah fill his glass from the jug set on the balcony wall. She came and went, her arms young and white, filling his stomach with food and giving him drink until he was satisfied. The girl came to him with a little pot of coffee, lifted up his plate and took it away. He contemplated the curve of her rump and the lines of her underwear under her thin housedress, this city sight strange amid the crudeness of the country. They had brought her here to marry her to any fool from Mahallat al-Gayad. Who deserved this lovely, graceful thing? He drained the last of his coffee and got up unhurriedly. Now, he knew, she was making his bed, and he passed from the salon into the bedroom, breathing quickly, the frenzy of his lust almost making him light-headed. He closed the bedroom door behind him and hugged the girl—she straightened up in a panic, but he pulled her to the bed with the heft of his body, his hands exploring her soft back under her dress. He pulled the dress over her head and rolled his head around in her breasts. He pulled down her panties and opened her thighs forcibly, and drew his member out of his underpants. It was not hard enough, but he thrust it despairingly into her vagina, to no avail. With a sudden burst of force the girl escaped from him and began to run; he got up, panting, full of contempt for himself, straightened his clothing, and went out. The girl will talk to my wife the Haja, he thought, and the Haja will slap her around, insult her; and he himself would stand abjectly before her.★ He went down the stairs. The butler, Saadawi, stood waiting to admit him, and on the radio he could hear the voice of Sheikh Mustafa Ismail chanting, " 'So Moses struck him with his fist, and killed him.' "★

"Bullshit!" shouted the mayor irritably. He switched off the radio crossly, muttering to himself. "What kind of man can be killed with a fist?"

He sat down in his big armchair and crossed his legs. Saadawi the coffee boy stood before him, humble and afraid. The mayor gazed at him and then spoke sarcastically.

"You're standing there like an idol. God damn you. Make me some coffee."

The boy sped off like an arrow, and the mayor stayed still as he sat for a few moments, then got up and went to his darkened office room. It smelled like dirt. He walked in the dark to his wardrobe and took out a bottle of cognac, filled

★*Haja* is the feminine form of the title *Haj*. It designates a devout Muslim who has made the pilgrimage to Mecca.
★Koran 28.15. The passage recounts the story of Moses' murder of the Egyptian who was fighting the Hebrew (told in Exod. 2:11–13).

its cap three times and drank it down, then put the bottle back in the wardrobe and went back to his big armchair. He sat down looking serious, and while he thought absently of the liquor coursing through his body, Fatimah came to him with a printed handkerchief.

"Here you are, sir."

He looked up at her; he could read affection in her eyes, and he felt tenderly toward her.

"Go away!" he shouted.

He did not want her to go, but she went away quietly. Saadawi brought in a little table and set the coffee beside the mayor, then disappeared quickly. The major began drinking his coffee. From a distance, Saadawi called out warily.

"Mr. Talaat, Abu Hanna, and Ali Effendi, scribe of the village council!"

"Send them in," said the mayor, without looking up.

Their entrance filled the still air of the room with noise. The mayor motioned them to sit with a slack movement of his hand. He felt small before their commanding stature and broad shoulders.

"The mission makes progress every day, thanks to the help of the mayor," said Talaat.

"Thank you," murmured the mayor.

Ali Effendi waved his arm as if he were onstage.

"As God is my witness—and I am a newcomer to this town—no one can deny what the mayor has done for us. This is what Niazi Effendi and I were discussing in the council. We never get tired of repeating it."

The mayor was stealing glances toward the doorway to

see whether Fatimah bint Abu Asakir might come back. Suddenly he realized that Ali Effendi had finished speaking, so he nodded.

"Thank you."

Talaat spoke up hastily.

"Ali Effendi, you are no newcomer here, you're one of us."

"Of course," the mayor agreed.

Ali Effendi resumed his stage declamation.

"And God is my hope—this is what gave me the nerve to come along with Talaat today to see you, after your concern for that Christian, the umbrella maker, whose landlady—one of his own religion—pitilessly threw him into the street."

So this is why they came, the mayor said to himself. Saadawi should have told me something about that at the beginning. He looked back at Talaat, who picked up where Ali had left off.

"The mission has decided to take an interest in the man. Muslims are enjoined to be kind to the People of the Book and to incline their hearts to Islam.★ So we have made a comprehensive campaign for all people to have their umbrellas repaired by that man or to buy new umbrellas from him. We have set a price, with no discount or rises. On top of that, we have a campaign to collect donations of money,

★The People of the Book, in Islam, are the recipients of divinely revealed scriptures before the advent of Islam: Jews and Christians. Most Shiite Muslim scholars in Iran also regard the monotheistic Zoroastrians as People of the Book.

food, and clothing, which will be reckoned and classified and delivered to him. The important thing is that this matter is now the main thing on our minds—everyone in the whole town is in on this."

Talaat paused to catch his breath, and Ali Effendi looked at him admiringly. The mayor looked around distractedly, and there was a moment of silence. A Coptic umbrella maker, said the mayor to himself; one of the People of the Book, whom they want to incline to Islam; the mission, the village council, the whole town; a mouse fallen from the rafters. They will play with him until the blood runs out of his nose, or dress him up like a boy scout and march him bare-kneed through the town, shouting, *Allahu akbar.*

Ali Effendi broke the silence.

"The truth is, Mr. Mayor, sir, the man is staying at my home, and that is fine with me—even if he stays forever. I'm just afraid it will embarrass him or bother him. So we were thinking that if he could get some little place to live, it would be better. We thought that the best thing might be Fakiha bint Tarawah's house."

"It's small and charming," said Talaat. "It is also near the mosque and the mission."

"The mosque and the mission?" the mayor asked quickly, not bothering to conceal his sarcasm.

"Talaat means that these are two places where there are people," Ali Effendi explained. "This artisan has to be where the people are."

"That's what I meant," said Talaat.

The woman who owned the house in question had died

leaving no family or heirs; the mayor compiled an inventory of the estate and sent it to the Islamic Court. The house was judged to be the property of the state treasury, and the executor sold it publicly, with only the mayor present; he pounced on it, as he had with many other properties, at a rather low price.

"Saadawi," the mayor said, "tell Mukhtar the watchman to give them the key to Fakiha bint Tarawah's house, and tell Sheikh Hasan the telephone operator to draft a rental agreement in Ali Effendi's name for thirty piasters per month, for three months."

The two men thanked the mayor and left. With the utmost hatred, he watched their backs recede.

"People cannot abide trouble. Not even one in forty thousand. Horrible."

His depression left him as he gazed through the half-open door, hoping for a glimpse of Fatimah.

*M*aster Awadallah could not sleep at night. He was beset by a sort of waking faint, in which nightmares and terrifying dreams opened his eyes in a deathlike stare. Then he would close his eyes again, but as soon as light first glowed in the window, he got up, fetched his bag, looked around cautiously, and was immediately absorbed in his work. Fula rose, sitting where she had been sleeping, gathering up her black clothes, winding them on her feet and head, sending her husband tender glances from under her eyelids. He was getting skinnier every day, his face was growing paler, and his eyes seemed to grow bigger. When Fula looked at him now, she saw his bones under his robe and inside his sleeves and was filled with anguish. The master sewed the cloth for the shade of the umbrellas, not raising his eyes to Fula, though he knew she was watching him, cradling him, and her heart wept. They loved each other from the day he first saw her as he sat before the house of her father, the church deacon in Kafr Sulayman Yusuf, the center of Mit Ghamr. He was still just a youth. His father had been crippled by illness.

"My son," he told him, "now you have sharp eyes and nimble fingers, and I am tired. Take the bag. Hang the umbrellas over your arm like a true artisan, and go out to my customers. You will please me if you do that."

He set out across the country, to Kafr Sulayman Yusuf among other places, where he sat in front of the deacon's house and saw her, and from that day he set out with his bag from their house in Azbat Ghali in Mit Ghamr. She was all he saw; he went around to his customers and came back again, and she was all he could think of. This went on for long years: he did not lift his eyes to hers, though he knew she was looking at him; he did not speak to her, though he knew that she bore the cares of his heart. When making a living in Mit Ghamr became hard for them, they said good-bye to their friends and moved on to Tanta. Once again living grew hard, and again they left, but what troubled him now was a strange thing that he had never foreseen. He recalled his father's face as he lay on his deathbed, and the face of Mrs. Gabuna, her soft voice filled with grief.

"Jesus Christ, Son of God, deliver us," she whispered.

Ali Effendi knocked at the door of the room and entered in a rampage.

"Good morning, sir! Look at you, hard at work before the birds are up! That's a real blessing, as we say. Sheikh Sayid al-Hasari and I said the dawn prayer together and had some coffee. If I had known you were up, I would have had you join us, but there's still coffee, and you and I will be drinking lots of coffee together."

Awadallah did not know what to say in reply to this speech of Ali Effendi's. He mechanically murmured, "Yes, of course, oh, fine," without really knowing what was being said to him, but the two children fidgeted and cried on the reed mat. Fula turned to comfort them, and Ali Effendi asked what was wrong with them. "Nothing," Fula said, but he came closer, and with his expert eye saw that both their bodies were covered with boils. Fula tried to hide them from him, but he addressed her in a loud voice, as if onstage.

"Don't be afraid. Let me probe them with my hand. I'm very used to children. Our house in town has more children than chickens or ducks, lambs, goats, or calves. The court-yard of the house is so full of all these species that you don't know where to step! I was used to children even before I was married, and then afterward, of course, too. Don't be afraid. Let me see. Aha! I have some very wholesome medicine for that."

He got up and found a tube of ointment and dressed all the boils while the children kept sobbing; but then they abruptly stopped and turned around. Awadallah and Fula turned, and so did Ali Effendi; heavy, decisive footsteps sounded from the courtyard of the house—it sounded like a company of soldiers. There was a knock at the door, and Brother Talaat entered, with a small group of young men of the Muslim Brotherhood, all strong, slim, and good-looking, with powerful shoulders and necks, each with the dark callous of frequent prayer on his forehead and a Brotherhood book in his hand. Their robes were clean, and the sandals on their feet shone; their presence proclaimed unity and obedience, and they gazed at Awadallah and Fula with wonder and delight. Brother Talaat spoke.

"The house of Fakiha bint Tarawah is ready at last, after the Brotherhood's long days of work, and now they have come to move Brother Awadallah into it."

"I was hoping that Awadallah would be staying with us for good," said Ali Effendi regretfully.

Awadallah did not understand what was going on and did not know what to say. The young men started picking things up to carry them away, and spontaneously, without thinking or understanding, he began to gather together his work tools and put them in the bag.

"This mat, this bed, everything in this room, all of it belongs to Brother Awadallah," said Ali Effendi.

Awadallah did not know what he should say.

"On behalf of the Muslim Brotherhood, thank you, Ali Effendi," Talaat announced.

They left the house carrying all the items. Among them was Awadallah, with his bag over his shoulder, and Fula with a bundle on her head and a child by each hand. Ali Effendi watched the procession recede.

"Where are they taking Uncle Awadallah, Daddy?" sobbed Attiyah.

"To a new house, son," Ali Effendi comforted him.

Master Awadallah tried to follow the steps of the handsome guards, trying to show his goodwill. Fula and the children walked behind, their sallow, sick faces fixed on the man walking before them, seeing nothing else in the world at this moment. He was ready to collapse in anguish. Brother Talaat led the group of young Brothers as they tramped methodically along, proclaiming greetings to passersby in hearty military tones and receiving clear and strong responses. From the doorways of houses, the women doused the road with water to settle the dust, waiting patiently for the procession to pass before stepping out, perplexed, to marvel at it. The men tightened their fists on their animals' reins and watched the procession with exultant but silent satisfaction. A powerful, vehement spirit had penetrated their hearts; as Talaat wished peace upon all of them, he was testing that spirit, and seeing that it was indeed clear and strong, he marched resolutely.

"Please come in."

Master Awadallah stepped into the house and stood in the courtyard silently. He did not know what to do. Fula stood beside him, holding hands with the children. The Brothers put down the household effects they were carrying and stood in a semicircle around the master, and now Talaat addressed Awadallah and Fula both.

"This is your new house, and we beseech God to bless

you in it. Now we'll move along and leave you, but before we leave, we would like to present you with a gift, in the name of the Muslim Brotherhood of Mahallat al-Gayad. Here it is—God's book. I hope you will accept it happily."

Talaat held out a printed book, and Awadallah held out his hands and accepted the book as he stood there. Talaat pointed to a marker in the book.

"We hope you'll read this part first."

"I will read it. I will read it," said Awadallah.

Another Brother stepped forward, very eager and excited, and set some books in a niche in the wall.

"These are the memoirs of our greatest spokesman for the Muslim Brotherhood, and some books by the great al-Ghazali, and some accounting forms."

They all said good-bye and left Awadallah standing where he was, holding the book in his hands. Then, exhausted, he fell on to the bench behind him. He closed his eyes for a few seconds as the three faces watched him in silence.

"Let's leave, Awadallah," Fula whispered. "Let's get out of here."

"It's too late, Fula," he said. "It's too late."

He opened his eyes and looked at the place where Talaat had pointed out the marker. The script in which the book was printed was unfamiliar to him and read with difficulty.

Didst thou say unto mankind, Take me and my mother as gods beside God? He saith: Be glorified! It was not mine to utter that which I had no right. If I used to say it, then Thou knewest it.

Thou knowest what is in my mind, and I know not what is in Thy mind. Lo! Thou, only Thou, art the Knower of hidden things. I spake unto them only that which Thou commandedest me . . . ⋆

The master could read no further. He rested his head against the wall behind him, and tears streamed down his face as he whispered:

"Jesus Christ, Son of God, may Your name be glorified."

The wording of the prayer was more than he could take . . . more than he could take.

The food at Uncle Ali Effendi's house was always excellent, and Abd al-Aziz ate his fill of fried eggs and beans in oil; now he dipped a big morsel of bread in white honey and cream and munched it with luscious, greedy pleasure. The house was clean and covered with morning dew. They were sitting at a table in the little courtyard; Ali's wife and daughters had rolled out reed mats and were sitting at a wide, low tray. On a shelf on the wall was a radio, with Sheikh Mustafa Ismail spreading a festive mood with his melodious chanting of the morning Koran selection. Abd al-Aziz ate with gusto, and Attiyah spoke to Uncle Ali Effendi.

"The table is for men and the tray is for women, right, Papa?"

"Yes, yes, yes," replied Ali Effendi delightedly.

Attiyah continued:

⋆Koran 5.116.

"We are men, right, Papa?"

Abd al-Aziz laughed, and the girls on the floor laughed.

"Yes, yes, yes," recited Uncle Ali Effendi.

"I'm a man, too, right, Papa?"

Abd al-Aziz collapsed laughing, as did the girls on the floor. Uncle Ali Effendi spoke up theatrically, though his wife sat stony-faced.

"You are a great man, Attiyah!" He added seriously, "Let's drink our tea and get down to business. We have lots of work to do today." He turned to Abd al-Aziz.

"I'll be back from Tanta this afternoon."

"I'll come with you," said Abd al-Aziz.

"Fine."

They walked through the neighborhood, up to Fakiha bint Tarawah's house. Uncle Ali Effendi pushed the door open and they went in, Abd al-Aziz behind him and looking in over his shoulder. The house was crowded with young men from the Brotherhood, and Master Awadallah sat in the midst of them, pale-faced, very thin, his eyes bulging. The Brothers made room for the visitors.

"There is no god but God—peace upon you, Sheikh Awadallah al-Mahdi!" was Ali's greeting.

"And peace upon you," replied Awadallah, his eyes wandering.

Talaat drew Abd al-Aziz aside to rouse him from his distraction, and greeted him. They shook hands warmly, but Abd al-Aziz was still distracted and preoccupied.

"How are things at the mission?" he asked Talaat.

"Never better," said Talaat enthusiastically. "I'm in charge now, and, God willing, I'll be doing most of the work."

"Oh," said Abd al-Aziz.

The lines of Talaat's face laughed.

"Today we're announcing his conversion in the Islamic Court."

"I've heard the story," Abd al-Aziz hesitated. "But he looks sick, doesn't he? He's so pale."

"Faith has lit up his face," smiled Talaat.

"Really? Strange."

The procession moved outside. Abd al-Aziz noticed the wife standing in the far corner with her two children, all three faces ashen and staring in terror, and his heart skipped a beat. They went out into the alley, where the ascending sun had still not burned off the morning dew, and the procession, led by the master flanked by Talaat and Ali Effendi, got underway. The rest followed behind, energetically greeting the people, who clamored their greetings back. Some of the crowd, carried away by zeal, shouted greetings to the master and then cried, *Allahu akbar!*

Others embraced him and pounded him on the back, while some of the women kissed his hand and asked him to pray for them. The master obligingly gave them his hand and murmured inaudibly. Abd al-Aziz never took his eyes off of him. It was like a market day: every moment they saw people slaughtering calves or sheep. The animals fought and kicked, but the blood spouted out of their throats. Some people had done their sacrificing early and hung the carcasses up by their doors. Some were still inflating their animals and hitting their bodies with sticks, while all the people around the animals shouted with joy. The procession moved out of the town and proceeded down the street, on its way up to the station. The shouts of the people still filled Abd al-Aziz's ears, and the din of sticks hitting the animals' swollen bodies. They boarded the train, the master flanked by Talaat and Ali Effendi; Abd al-Aziz was at a good distance but did not take his eyes off the man. He noticed that there was a youth from the Brotherhood standing beside him, whose face burned with zeal. He looked at him listlessly—the food he had gobbled at breakfast was now a weight within him, as his stomach soured and filled with gas. The boy spoke to him.

"Brother—"

"Abd al-Aziz."

"You are one of the Brothers, of course."

"I used to be."

"Why did you quit?"

"Maybe I wasn't lucky."

"Man seeks God—he doesn't ask God to seek him."

"You are right."

"Have you read this?" He held up the book *Thus We Learn* in his hand.

"Not yet. I've had it for some time, though."

"Do you fill out an accounting form before you go to sleep?"

"To tell you the truth, no."

"That's strange. I can never fall asleep until I've looked

back on my day and written down my sins on the form, then asked God to forgive me for them. *Then* I can sleep."

"I haven't slept very well for a long time anyway."

"You have to repent and start over."

Abd al-Aziz was silent a while before asking the young Brother, "Did you help guide this man into Islam?"

"We all did."

"Was it very hard?"

"From the time the man first came to our town, until this morning, we never let up for a moment."

"That's impressive."

"For the important occasion, we're organizing a big religious symposium in town, and we'll invite Brother Said and all the branches in the area."

"Great."

"Yes, Brother, Islam is on the march, thanks to young people who believe in their Lord, and the guidance we give them."

"Oh. But the torn, confused ones, nothing marches on thanks to them?"

"What's that? I don't understand."

"Just a thought, never mind. Now we're in Tanta."

At the station, the procession disembarked amid throngs of country people with their luggage and children, flowing out into the shabby streets of the old city. Abd al-Aziz seized Ali Effendi's hand, his heart pounding.

"I'm thinking of going back to the village now."

"Brother, you only spent the night at my house."

"I know, but I really want to go back."

"God!"

"I'm sorry, but I'm uncomfortable here."

"Was anything wrong at my house?"

"Good God, no, I'm more at home in your house than I am in my father's."

"So?"

"I just haven't felt very well the last few days."

"As you like."

"Thank you, to you and my aunt."

"God forgive me, as if you have to thank us! Remember me to your other uncles and aunts."

"Of course, God willing. I just want to tell Talaat."

Talaat tugged at his arm.

"I'm sorry you won't be able to stay for our celebration."

"I'm the sorry one, but there's nothing I can do." Then he said, "I want to say hello to this man."

Abd al-Aziz went to the master, whose eyes were wandering so that he seemed to be seeing practically nothing, and took his warm, sweaty hand. Abd al-Aziz contemplated his face and wanted to say something. He embraced him, but the words stuck in his throat. He shook his hand cordially, then let go of it slowly so that it would not drop. He turned toward the whole crowd and passed through the mass of bodies, seeing nothing, not hurrying, letting himself be carried by the currents of moving people, saying to himself, "This has to stop. This has to stop." Still wandering, he screamed to himself, "I have to intervene and stop it myself!" He looked at his watch: three hours had passed since he left the people. The thing must be completely over by now. He closed his eyes and shook his head.

"How horrible it is to realize something too late, after everything's ruined! How horrible! I'm sorry!"

$\mathcal{S}$ubhi Muhammad came from a wretchedly poor family living in al-Milaygi Alley, which opened onto Taha Hakim Street in Tanta. His father was a vicious drunkard, and his brothers were all afflicted with osteomalacia. They had bow-legs and very bad teeth; even as children they had the faces of senile old men. Their mother was fat, very pale and afraid, and spent her whole day cooking or washing clothes, with Subhi at her side. He was extremely handsome, with a girlish face, full and rather pale. His hair was thick, glossy, and black, and he oiled, parted, and combed it with extreme care. Gentle, soft-spoken Subhi helped his mother with the housework all day long, and if there was nothing he could do to help her, he sat with his school texts and notebooks, and no one heard a sound out of him. He was calm and quiet in class, too, but his teachers knew him to be hard-working and organized in everything. His silence, absorption, and pallor kept him aloof from the students at the Tanta Secondary School; his care for his clothes and fastidious elegance made of the distance between him and his schoolmates a shield of dignity. Religious affairs were nearly unknown in their house and, indeed, were never even mentioned, so godliness just did not cross Subhi's mind. But the Muslim Brotherhood group at his school appealed to him, with their earnestness and love for one another. He went to Othman, their representative at the school, a boy with with an aristocratic forehead and a part in his curly hair, who spoke to him gently and affectionately.

"Brother, God has revealed His scripture, and all we want is for God's word to rule over our world as it rules over our faith, and Brother, our world will be better for it."

Subhi had never heard any words that touched him as profoundly as these or put a look of such unaccustomed luxurious ease on his face, but his life had now found an explanation, a pattern, an image. He took the Brotherhood's books home with him, put them among his schoolbooks, and began to read them, peacefully but eagerly. He did not pray in the house, so as not to cause any problem; he went out to the mosques at a time when it would neither attract attention nor anger or depress his mother. He missed some of the set prayer times but said to himself that God knew and forgave. He performed the prayers according to the way they were described in his schoolbooks, without embellishment or ceremony.

When he saw Brother Said for the first time, giving a speech in a crowded tent in the Tanta town square, he became infatuated with him: he was good-looking and wore a Pakistani sort of skullcap on his head; he had connections with the Islamic state of Pakistan. When Said spoke, he won over the whole audience. He cursed them for their abandonment of God's word, which he described in wounding terms, until the people were torn with regret, but he told them about the youths who believed in their Lord, and filled them with purpose: these youths were knights by day but monks by night. When he read from the Koran, he gave them gooseflesh—they were filled with humiliation and remorse, but he assured them that the gate of repentance was still open and urged them to lose no time in finding God. After this sermon, Subhi saw nothing else in the world but Brother Said's lovely face. He went home quietly and went to sleep, but thereafter began to buy the monthly magazine Said published and read every word he wrote in that magazine or any other. When he went to visit relatives in Cairo, the first thing he did his first morning was to go to the magazine's office in El-Nil Street and ask to meet the Brother who lived on an upper floor of that building. After a short wait he was permitted to go up. Brother Said was sitting at his desk, wearing a *robe de chambre* over a white galabia; his face and his hair still looked as if he were asleep. Subhi sat down silently, but when Brother Said murmured, "Yes, Brother," in a friendly voice, the power of speech returned to him. He talked about Said's articles and how much he loved reading them. Said liked him and smiled at him, saying, "God bless you, Brother." And then he said, "I'm meeting with the Brotherhood tonight, God willing, in Daher. I would be happy to have you there, Brother Subhi."

Subhi walked back satisfied, knowing what might happen for the first time in his life. At the meeting in Daher, the Brotherhood all sat on reed mats after the evening prayer, Brother Said stood among them, and they all listened until after midnight. Said had not forgotten Subhi, however, and after the meeting, he told him, "Welcome, Brother Subhi."

He shook his hand, patted him on the back, said good-
night to the Brothers who were at the door to see him off,
and waved to them as he walked to his car. He motioned for
Subhi to get in and slid in behind the steering wheel. The
small car sped off, driven expertly and confidently by Said,
who was smiling, though his brown forehead shone with
nobility and the burden of responsibility. The car flew to
Heliopolis, where the wide streets were neat and well lit,
with very few pedestrians. This was a Cairo Subhi had never
seen. They mounted the steps of a building with an immense
glass door and a gleaming elevator, and the apartment was as
huge as a palace, with wonderfully elegant men talking in
soft voices and laughing pleasantly. They embraced Said
warmly.

"It's good to see you," he said to one of them.

"Anything for the Brotherhood," the man replied.

"Shall we make a move into my office?" he asked them.

Some of the group stood up and followed them. Among
them was a very earnest and dignified man. The ones who
stayed were friendly to Subhi, asked him questions, moved a
platter of almonds, nuts, and cake closer to him, and gave
him a glass of tamarind juice. He ate avidly, because he was
hungry, and followed their conversation closely but in silence. A long time after, Brother Said came out, shook their
hands, and embraced them. Then Subhi and Said hurried
out, and the car flew off once again. The air was heavy with
the silence that comes before dawn, and from the Cairo min-
arets resounded the humble entreaties that precede the call to
prayer.

"Let's say the morning prayer in the al-Rawdah Mosque," said Said.

After the prayer, Said said to Subhi, "I don't think you're going back to your relatives, Brother Subhi. Sleep with me, dear Brother."

They entered the magazine office, where Subhi was delighted to find a bedroom. He was concerned lest Said awaken his wife and children on his account, but Said pointed to the bed and said, "It's a small bed, but it's enough for us. We can rest for an hour."

He gave Subhi a clean white nightshirt, and they climbed into the bed. The room was quiet, and Said spoke in his deep voice about the Caliph Omar ibn al-Khattab.

"If someone like him ruled this country," he whispered, "he could bring the people around."

Then there was more silence.

"Tell me about yourself, Brother Subhi."

Subhi did not want to say anything. He was experiencing a moment of profound pleasure and did not want to spoil it, even with his own breathing. He said nothing, and Said said, very feelingly:

"You are gorgeous, Brother Subhi."

Then he leaned into him and hugged him to his chest, and Subhi responded with his eyes closed. His soft chest rested on Said's slender, muscular chest; everything in Subhi was calm and gratified. Said kissed him on the lips with a kiss full of Islamic love and brotherhood, and thus they slept until daybreak. Thereafter, they met whenever Subhi came to Cairo or Said came to Tanta; they shared a great affection.

One evening there was a packed meeting in a huge tent in the Tanta town square, which lasted until after midnight, and after it, the senior Brothers gathered around Brother Said on the roof of the mission headquarters in the clock-tower square. When dawn approached, people began to leave, but a small group stayed around Brother Said, among them Subhi and Talaat, who had come from Mahallat al-Gayad with a delegation of young men from the mission.

"Masses of the Brotherhood will be waiting for you when you come to us tomorrow, Brother Said," said Talaat.

"Yes, God willing," said Said.

Talaat smiled his best smile.

"The Brotherhood is very excited about the proclamation of Brother Awadallah al-Mahdi's conversion to Islam."

Everyone gaped at Talaat, overwhelmed.

"Thanks to God's grace, and your great effort, Brother Talaat." Said leaned toward Subhi. "Have you ever been to Mahallat al-Gayad before, Brother Subhi?"

"No," said Subhi softly.

Subhi clasped his shoulder affectionately.

"We'll go together, God willing."

"You will all be our honored guests," said Talaat generously.

Ali Effendi performed the sundown prayer on the white mat adorned with scenes of city life, which had been a present from Sheikh Sayid al-Hasari, but he could not concentrate his mind on the prayer. He was distracted and disturbed, though he did not know the reason. The breath of the town reached him, redolent of boundless noise and violence as they celebrated the conversion of Awadallah al-Mahdi to Islam. Delegations of Muslim Brotherhood youths were pouring in from neighboring towns, and their shouts of *Allahu akbar* resounded. The local Brotherhood was welcoming him with the same cries. He could hear the car horns and the roar of the loudspeakers broadcasting Brother Said's speech to the throngs. This was not the first time all this had happened in the town, but today his spirit was troubled, and he did not know why. He got up as usual to go and say the evening prayer in the Friday mosque; there he would meet some of the Brothers of the Path. After the prayer, they went together to the house of Sheikh Sayid al-Hasari. He said good-bye to his wife and asked Attiyah to be the man of the house until he got back. He left the house and went out into the neighborhood, where the town's clamor was even louder than before. No one was walking slowly—they pounded the earth with their feet and filled the air with their hoarseness. He calmly told his prayer beads and walked cautiously through the gloomy darkness, recognizing Talaat and some of the other Brothers surrounding Awadallah al-Mahdi. They were all standing around him and greeting the master.

"How are you, Sheikh Awadallah? How are you, Mahdi?"

He did not hear the man make any reply. He seemed dazed: his face was dead and his eyes were stuporous, even crazed. Like lightning the question flashed in his mind,

"What has happened?" He could not control his conversation with Talaat, who asked him:

"Where are you headed, Ali Effendi?"

"To the mosque to say the evening prayer, God willing," he said, like a sleepwalker. He could not take his eyes off of Awadallah.

Talaat was surprised.

"Brother Said has called on everyone to go and pray in his mosque on the plaza in the middle of town. What's with you?"

Ali Effendi was still distracted, watching Awadallah closely.

"I'm going to the mosque. I'll see my friends there and we'll go to our Sufi meeting. It's Friday night."

Talaat shook his head.

"We would like to have you with us."

They said good-bye and the others left, leaving Ali Effendi standing stock-still looking at their backs, holding Awadallah by his arms, their feet stomping the ground. "What has happened?" The question wrung his heart. Was this why Abd al-Aziz had left town, leaving his uncle's house when all this was beginning? He walked along slowly, fingering his prayer beads, careful not to bump into any of the wild pedestrians around him. So he had converted to Islam? He sighed, unable to understand. Yet they had guided the man to the true faith, to which we all belong. Still, his heart was full of fear. He asked God to give him refuge from Satan. In the mosque he performed the ablutions again; he did not know whether his previous ablutions were still valid or whether he had lost the ritual state of purity on his way here. After the prayer, he and Sheikh al-Hasari went out into the darkness of the town; the Sheikh was still murmuring supplications, and Ali Effendi listened gravely. The confusion of moving shapes, noises, and the flash of torches disoriented the nearsighted Sheikh, so he grasped Ali Effendi's upper arm.

"Take my arm, Ali Effendi."

Ali Effendi in turn took the man's arm as the Brotherhood marched behind them. The old man whispered:

"There is no power and no strength save in God—this looks like Resurrection Day. They think this spectacle will substitute for their religious duties."

They walked along in their wary, whispering rhythm, amid the convulsive rhythm of the air of the town, and arrived at Sheikh Sayid al-Hasari's house, a house with a large courtyard where bundles of rush mats and stalks stood in the corners; the ground was covered with new rush mats that still needed to be trod down before their final stitching.

"These will be good for our meeting—they're the best thing, and clean."

They all sat around a long, low, narrow table upon which some small lamps were placed. Loudspeakers carried in Brother Said's speech, but they began their recitations, and Ali Effendi closed his eyes so that neither his apprehensions nor the loud commotion outside would distract him from the reading. After the recitation came the prayers for the dead, for the early Muslims, and for all their absent brethren, of this world and the next, but a certain tension infected everything. Ali Effendi broke the silence that had fallen by speaking aloud unintentionally.

"They're celebrating for Sheikh Awadallah al-Mahdi."

"Oh," muttered Sheikh Sayid al-Hasari.

This mutter stopped Ali Effendi cold, but he continued as if to anticipate the others.

"This was really a good omen for Islam, by God."

Sheikh Sayid al-Hasari spoke slowly.

"This big commotion makes hearts heavy and blinds perception. No man can see any good in it at all."

"These are people who read the Koran," said Ali Effendi, as if evading his own apprehensions.

"But this spectacle denies the wisdom of what they read, and their vehemence has the savor of coercion."

"Coercion?" asked Ali Effendi bewilderedly.

"Yes, my brother, I see coercion in their spectacle," said Sheikh Sayid al-Hasari in his calm voice, which had never sounded so absolute and decisive. "I see coercion when your brother greets you in a voice louder than is needed for you to hear him, to test your intention toward him. I see it when someone invites a guest to shame him, to prevent him from refusing. I see it when a wrongdoer overdoes his apologies, to shame the man he has wronged out of showing his pain. I see coercion in all these cases. In all of them I can see coercion."

"The man was not coerced," said Ali Effendi in despair. "He chose Islam voluntarily."

"Yes," said Sheikh Sayid al-Hasari, his voice trembling, "I see coercion here, and I see weak people being subjected to torture."

Silence fell. The men sat with their heads bowed, the loudspeakers blaring over their heads. This was more than Ali Effendi could stand; he had to say something.

"Sheikh Sayid, the man was not coerced into committing some crime, after all. He found his way to God."

The Sheikh paused uncertainly before saying slowly:

"His way. I do not know if it was his way."

"You don't know?" asked Ali Effendi worriedly. "You do not know, Sheikh Sayid?"

"Yes, I do not know," the Sheikh answered firmly. "But I believe that God's servant finds his path to godliness through a Lord that he knows, with whom he is content, and whom he loves. Yes. A Lord he knows, with whom he is content, and whom he loves."

Ali Effendi trembled.

"Or is there more than one Lord, then, Sheikh Sayid?"

"There is no god but God, the Truth," said Sheikh Sayid al-Hasari quietly.

All the men repeated this formula, their faces confused and worried, but Ali Effendi persisted.

"So?"

The Sheikh nodded patiently and answered as timidly as a child.

"I am just a humble maker of mats, and I do not know. Let us read the opening prayer so that God may enlighten us and open our eyes, my brothers. Things have become ambiguous."

They read the prayer in whispers, with the sound of the loudspeakers reverberating triumphantly over their soft whispers. Then they all had to part, each taking with him his luck from the melancholy of the path. Ali Effendi wished that he could stay with Sheikh Sayid al-Hasari until the voice of God heralded the morning, but he knew that could not be; that he would have to go and lie in his room all alone, never closing his eyes, staring into the blackness and gaining no understanding from it; and the cold of fear stole into his bones.

$\mathcal{B}$rother Talaat had asked permission to bring Brother Said and a group of senior Muslim Brotherhood officials to pay their respects to the mayor, but that was more than the mayor could stand. He ordered that Talaat be told "The mayor is not in." Saadawi was surprised by this, but the mayor repeated his instructions and ordered him to put a little lamp in his office. He locked himself in, sat down in a big, cozy armchair, and took out his bottle of cognac. He poured himself a glass and drank it greedily. His whole belly burned. He hated—loathed—his wife and had lived with this hatred for twenty-five years. The hatred had utterly weakened him. Why had he done it to himself? Why had he not divorced her years ago? How had the years gone by, leaving him mute, a spectator? Now he was an exile on the second floor, hardly ever seeing her. He saw her only when she wanted to find fault with him or scold him. He would listen quietly and then go up to his bedroom or pass by his office. How had he wasted his life in this way? Why did he not divorce her now? Why did he have to be banished to the second floor, to lurk in corners for the maids? They resisted him, they pushed his hands away from their breasts and buttocks, then ran off to tell his wife. They knew that she ruled over him, that she insulted and humiliated him. It pained him to his deepest soul to be humiliated that way, but he always came back, came back in a recurrent circle of abuse. But now there was this Fatimah bint Abu Asakir; she had not said anything to his wife, and he did not know why. She was around him all day, and he tried to find out; he tried to read the expression on her face but found nothing but that silent, sympathetic smile in her eyes. This wounded him to his marrow, but he had become despicable—so despicable that he had become no better than trash.

The sound of the loudspeaker reverberated dreadfully; he could not escape it. He filled his glass again. Who did those people want? The man had converted to Islam. What did they want now? They were convulsing the whole town; it was a convulsion he rejected, that drove him to silence; it denied and excluded all reason and wisdom; it was a pitiless scourge, this mass rush into the abyss. I feel my end is near, I can see it, I can even be certain of it. It will be in the next step I take. He drank until his eyes filled with tears and he felt the heaviness of his limbs; then the patches of light, blocks of shadow, and blurred forms disappeared. He tried to get up and felt his way to the door. He went up the stairs. All was silence, except for the terror looming over the rooftops of the town. He detested those people; he feared them but did not want to clash with them. He was disheartened and weary and went up the staircase slowly until he reached the second floor, where he came upon Fatimah bint Abu Asakir coming down. He stopped silent in front of her; now freed from her housekeeping duties, she was wearing a light night-gown. Perhaps intrigued by the loudspeakers, she had gone up to the roof to look. Her nightgown was not suited to this country night; she was virtually naked in it. Her white neck and shoulders were exposed; her hair hung down to her shoulders, and he could see the sublime, sympathetic smile in her narrow eyes, as well as her small, round breasts and the suggestion of her nipples. She looked at him, not hiding the aura of her being, not hesitating, not affected; she grew in pride and sublimity as his insignificance grew, until he nearly bent over to rub his forehead on the step where they stood. He turned on the step, opened the landing door that led to the rooms, and went inside, sensing her soundless steps be-hind him. He would have liked to run but could not; he nearly fell on his face but grasped the doorknob to hold himself up. The room was dark, but he found a light pene-trating from the lamp Fatimah was holding. She set it on the end table beside the bed and stood there silently.

The mayor could not move; she came closer to the clothes rack, took his nightshirt, held it in her hand, and stood in front of him. The mayor began to take his clothes off, like an obedient child, until he was completely naked and stood in front of her, ashamed. She watched, without batting an eyelash. He put on his nightshirt and went over to the bed, lay down, and pulled the coverlet over himself, even though the night was hot. He closed his eyes, burdened and dizzied by the liquor, then felt the weight of her body as she sat beside him on the bed. He did not open his eyes, afraid; he felt her hand move slowly under the coverlet and slip between his open thighs. She took his member in her fingers; it was just as limp as a rooster's comb. She played with it expertly but gently, and he realized that tears were rolling from under his closed eyelids and streaming down, warm and fast. Fatimah shifted and threw the coverlet off of him and got up on her hands and knees over his body. He felt the details of her body against his. She took his face in the palms of her small hands and wiped the tears from his eyes with her thumbs. He looked at her, and she smiled like a child. Like that, now, he perceived the abyss, just one step away, and now he was falling, falling—now what would Fatimah bint Abu Asakir do with him? His despair mingled with relief, the relief that death grants men.

"Father, the hour is come, the glory of Your Son, may Your Son also be glorified." This is what Master Awadallah shouted in a tremendous voice that no one could hear, none of those who had come to him, as he stood bareheaded and bare-chested in the courtyard of the house, in a simple woven nightshirt. His face was hot with fever, and a white froth collected at the corners of his mouth. His eyes were half closed: he did not see Talaat or the band of young Muslim Brotherhood men pushing open the door and entering, but behind his eyelids there was a black, black, clamorous, sorrowful vision of the church in Kafr Sulayman Yusuf, crowded with the people, with Father Andrus al-Bahidi celebrating mass and old Rizqallah, the deacon, behind him. His head was a confusion of the people's sad, tearful voices. The church was draped in black banners. None of those coming to greet him heard the terrible screaming that resounded within him. He could not speak.

"Peace upon you, Brother Awadallah al-Mahdi" was Talaat's greeting.

"Lo, the hour is approaching, when the Son of man is to be delivered over to his tormenters." This was the immense voice that resounded inside him, but not a word crossed his lips in response to the weeping of the people in the church. His wife, Fula, stood in the corner of the courtyard; she had pulled a black kerchief over her hair, her hands were clasped on her chest, and her eyes were lowered. She was flanked by Lawzah and Hantas; they were staring at the master's bare feet. One of the Brotherhood boys glanced at Talaat and whispered in terror:

"The man is ill—he's actually dying."

Talaat sucked his bloody saliva and scowled, twisting his face.

"First comes the show that all these masses of Brothers are expecting," he said resolutely. "After that, Brother, we'll take him to a doctor."

The boy said nothing more, and Talaat looked around, past the wife, Fula, and pointed to the master's clothes hanging on a nail in the wall.

"Bring those clothes, Brother."

The boy took them down hesitantly and brought them not to the master but to Talaat, who took them, giving two

Brothers a look that authorized them to assist him. The three then stepped forward and surrounded the feverish Awadallah, who gave them his body without the slightest resistance. He was trembling slightly, his lips moving with the tremendous screaming that resounded inside him, and none of those around him could hear. In his closed eyes the sorrowful scenes in the church of Kafr Sulayman Yusuf were being played out, as Father Andrus al-Bahidi celebrated the mass, with the deacon, old Rizqallah, giving the responses amid the people crying in the nave, which was draped in black cloth and saintly icons.

"We have to wrap this turban around his head," said Talaat firmly.

The great voice rang out: "The soldiers wove a crown of thorns, put it on his head, and threw a scarlet cloak around him." Talaat adjusted the turban on his head, looked at him, and laughed.

"You are a great man now, Awadallah al-Mahdi."

None of the Brothers returned his smile. Talaat smacked his lips and looked in the direction of Fula, then looked away. His eyes moved back, avoiding her, to settle on one of the Brothers.

"Go into that room and see where he left his shoes."

That boy brought the shoes and put them on the master's feet. Talaat held his right arm and gave the other Brother a glance for him to take his left arm. The feverish man was now utterly weary. His head was filled with the clamor of the church scene and the funeral rites. His screaming had not stopped, though no one heard it: "Then the soldiers, the commander, and the Jewish servants arrested Jesus and took him away." He was a stripped body in their hands. Without another look in Fula's direction they took him out, almost carrying him by his arms, his feet dragging on the ground. There was a throng of young people, women, and children at the gate of the house, and when he came into view they burst into shrieks, delighted trilling, and shouts of joy. Abruptly the bright daylight and the noise woke the master, and he came to slightly; he opened his eyes and his pace slowed. In his feverish nightmare, he imagined that these people were the weeping congregation in the church of Kafr Sulayman Yusuf. His face was bright with joy and fever. He smiled at them and raised his arm.

"Peace be upon you," he said.

Maddened with delight, the people were seized by the idea that this was one of God's righteous chosen, and they surged around him, trying to kiss his hand or his robe, to feel the savor of righteousness in his febrile, dreaming smile un-affected by the crazed shrieking. The young men of the Brotherhood had to form an unbreakable circle around him and bring him to their mission office.

On the steps of the mission stood a crowd of Muslim Brotherhood officials. Short, slim, and strong, Brother Said stood in their midst, wearing his little Pakistani cap. He stood tense and alert, his eyes brimming with intelligence and self-confidence. Brother Subhi stood at his side, looking pale and feminine, his hair full and combed, his gaze wandering. They were surrounded by a group of Brothers from the Tanta mission and the missions from around Mahallat al-Gayad. Each young man had on his head the dark brown mark of prayer. Most of them had the same look. They were united by a profound ethnic resemblance; their facial features advertised the same cold sullenness and severity. Most of them were wearing suits. Some wore overcoats over their robes; some wore turbans and some were bareheaded, but there was a general air of ferocity, spiritlessness, and mania. Talaat hurried up the steps and shook Brother Said's hand with a laugh, then shook hands with the rest, who joyfully greeted and kissed him. Then he stopped and pointed to Awadallah, who had not followed him up but stood proudly at the bottom of the steps, staring forward; Said immediately realized that the man was in a stupor, from illness of some sort, and would not come up to them. So he quickly went down to him; Said's action startled the rest of the Brotherhood officials out of their inertia, and they hurried down the steps after him. The master gave them his damp, feverish hand, murmuring, flecks of froth at the corners of his mouth. Each of them shook his hand and went back up to where they had been standing. At that moment, a youth in a boy-scout uniform, with a kerchief around his neck and stripes on his shoulder that identified him as the troop leader for Mahallat al-Gayad, climbed the steps and shook the Brothers' hands, then stood beside them and gave the signal to begin. The loudspeaker started up.

"The Muslim Brotherhood scout troop of Mahallat al-Gayad, forward, march."

The drums began to beat a military rhythm, and the scouts' chapped country legs set out marching in their shorts, threadbare socks, and every possible kind of shoe. They moved to the sound of the drums at a poor, disorganized pace. The faces of the poor country boys showed signs of malnutrition, and their hair was cut in the plain country way; their uniforms were khaki. After the rows of scouts came the Brotherhood, with flags and banners and the pounding drums; then a jeep full of Brothers with a loudspeaker, which they were using to broadcast their slogans and cries; then troops of visiting boy scouts. They were followed by the master, astride the mayor's white horse, whose bridle was held by one of the Brothers, while two more supported Awadallah from each side. Masses of peasants, their patience completely exhausted, fought to touch the master until they broke through the human wall that the strong young men of the Brotherhood had put up around him. The man was in a daze, his face resolutely forward under the blazing sun, the corners of his mouth still marked with white froth. In this order the procession wound through the town, raising clouds of dust, heading toward its end at the town mosque, where this Friday's communal prayers were to be held.

$\mathcal{T}$he mayor tiptoed warily down the stairs; he did not want his feet to make any sound; not even the sound of his own breathing reached his ears. He tried to guess which point the procession might have reached as it moved along its route, and when it would arrive at its final stop. A vague throb of fear seized his heart. He wished that Fatimah would never leave his sight for a second—no sooner had she turned her back and gone away than he was sick with longing for her. He did not want to cease feeling, even for a moment, the delight of obedience to her, of giving in to her caprices and mood changes. Fear had seized his heart; the rhythm of this chaos had convulsed the town to its roots. He did not see Saadawi anywhere. Furious, he almost cried from loneliness, like a child, and went into his office. He brought out his bottle and began to drink a series of glasses of cognac, until his thirst was quenched and his anxieties calmed. He sensed the procession approaching and imagined that they were coming with their drums to arrest him. With their drums they would drive him into a corner from which he could not escape. Then they would seize him, blindfold him, and throw his head against the back of his big chair. Tears welled up under his eyelids; in his darkness he could almost see the procession in the fire of the sun, amid clouds of dust; he could almost recognize the faces, one by one, and the people, man by man.

"What inferno," he whispered to himself, "what terrible plague or huge massacre or catastrophic earthquake is needed to make those people stop and look around them, to contemplate in silence what terror had wrought; then start afresh, more quietly, sadder, wiser, and more simply?"

His tears streamed down his face as the procession grew near.

"Saadawi!" he called from his chair. "Saadawi!"

Only silence met his call, and he felt alarm. He stood up, frightened, and looked out through the window blind.

The procession was just opposite. He saw the master's feverish face and froth-stained mouth, drew back quickly, and threw himself back into his chair, crying and cackling.

"Will they parade me like that, hanging over a donkey's back? Me and Fatimah, with my wife the Haja marching in front with a loudspeaker, shrieking out my shame?" He swallowed his tears, opened his eyes, and spoke calmly but firmly. "When that happens, I will be as proud and serene as that Copt."

And he went back to drinking the glasses that never satisfied him.

$\mathcal{A}$li Effendi finished his ablutions and dried his face with the white towel, which he tossed onto his daughter's shoulder as she stood obediently before him. She silently put away the pitcher and towel, then came back and lifted the basin while her father stood praying. His wife and childen knew the father's brooding silence and dared not say a word. At-tiyah was inevitably in his mother's room, watching his father warily. Ali Effendi took his prayer beads and left the house in silence. He knew that the procession was on the other side of town. He walked through neighborhoods that were empty except for a few women here and there, all of them talking about the wonderful qualities of the holy man Awadallah al-Mahdi. He kept walking until he reached the house of Sheikh Sayid al-Hasari. He pushed open the door and greeted the man sitting on the prayer mat. The man made room for him and they sat together.

"It is almost prayer time, Sheikh Sayid," said Ali Effendi. "Shall we put our faith in God and go to the Friday mosque?" Sheikh Sayid said nothing, but raised his dim-sighted gaze toward Ali Effendi. The sound of the commotion filled the air of the place, like a solid presence between them. They could not resume their conversation and could hardly see each other. Sheikh al-Hasari sighed and spoke sorrowfully.

"Today the town is not praying, it is holding this great lamentation for some reason that only God knows."

"Yes," said Ali Effendi sadly.

The Sheikh's voice rose, firm and sharp.

"All this noise deprives prayer of the reason for worship. I don't want any part of it."

"There is no god but God." Ali Effendi sounded pained.

Sheikh Sayid stood up purposefully.

"I am going out. I will look for some other town where people are praying today."

Ali Effendi followed him out quietly. They walked through the empty streets, listening to the last of the women's gossip. Ali Effendi sighed.

"Sheikh Sayid, I am in torment. Sheikh Sayid, I turned my guest over to them. If I spend my whole life praying, God will still never forgive my sin."

"Yes, yes," Sheikh Sayid al-Hasari quavered. "We all handed the man over. We all did it, Ali Effendi."

"Yes," sighed Ali Effendi.

"We handed him over," Sheikh Sayid al-Hasari continued. "And now we have no power over their madness."

They walked, silent and defeated, looking for another town in which to pray.

$\mathcal{T}$he procession approached the mosque, and the roar of the loudspeakers grew more agitated, the thumping of the drums grew more violent, and the tramping of the scouts' worn-out shoes grew more zealous. The persons crowded around the master grew more intense and frenzied, the dust storm grew denser, and the sun pounded the fire-heated nails in the master's forehead. He swayed on the horse. When they took him down at the gate of the mosque, he fell down on his face, completely unconscious. Like fire through straw, the cry "Al-Mahdi is dead!" spread through the crowd. Those around him sat him down on the ground, shook him, and massaged his temples, but to no avail. The ring of protective bodies around the master nearly broke, but suddenly they found that Fula had slipped through from the midst of the crowd and thrown herself on al-Mahdi. She held him to her breast, and in a moment, as if the roar of the crowd had sunk into a bottomless well, silence rang out profoundly. The people saw Fula hold the master to her breast and pray in agony.

"In the name of our Lord, Jesus Christ."

She made the sign of the cross on her breast.

Good News from
the Afterlife

$\mathcal{D}$ EATH

$\mathcal{A}$ great gate with a high, gloomy archway, simply ornamented, in a profoundly silent wall of white stone blocks covered with the dust of bygone ages. The door panels were of thick wood, filigreed with iron leaves studded with large-headed nails. The journey was predestined, the intention born in a moment of dark silence, with echoes that may have eluded his hearing but struck his heart. It still tweaked his taut skin until a fear arose—from scenes familiar and unfamiliar, from experiences remembered and others even before memory. It was a fear from which there was no escape, nor could it be shared with others, for they were too frightened even to see one another. One had to move along with it—as a wounded man moves along with his wound to seek healing—to wherever the fear might be healed.

The journey here passed through a narrow alley whose opposite sides were very close, blocking out between them the blazing sun, dust, and suffocating heat; life before the gates of the houses was foul, crippled, and haphazard, a life forgetful of its end, without any context, never stopping to catch its breath or to contemplate itself. In the houses, the women were sworn to renunciation, black clothes, weeping, and a suffocating subjugation they endured with black resentment and venomous rancor. The men sat habitually in the plaza at the head of the alley, the ground underneath them pulsing with the movement of the women in the courtyards of the houses. Can wise words and and fine sermons tame the terror? Can they break the spells cast on the hearts that yearn for the bloom of femininity and the bloom of manhood? What inexorable fate has seized the hearts of men and women?

The journey began at the plaza and passed through the alley to the rhythm of dolorous words in poems of patience and scenes of calamity, in tales of fate and destiny. Even at the end of the journey, this gate was anonymous among all the other gates, but if one observed it a little, he discovered that everything about it was different. The construction, intensely depressing, plunged the observer into silence, a sorrow that almost squeezed a tear out of the corner of his eye, but the gate—in spite of that—conveyed goodness and familiarity to the emotions. One did not know which detail in that severe construction imparted goodness; perhaps the iron door knocker in the shape of a lovely, delicate lady's hand clasping a little ball striking on an anvil carved into the door panel. An elegant arrangement in a setting of brooding majesty.

The grandson contemplated this arrangement until a smile of condolence bloomed in his heart and gave him determination. He pushed the door, and it opened with the hoped-for, if not expected, ease. But the grandson was silent and frightened. When he closed the door, behind it he found a small, open space, very neat and profoundly silent and dark. The hard mud walls were plain and smooth, the ceiling was made of reeds and the bark of palm trunks. To the right stood the door to an open room. His grandfather's shoes were on the threshold, with a neat scroll of faded kidskin. The adjacent pair were in two exactly parallel lines. The floor was entirely covered with yellow mats, faded from foot traffic. His grandfather was sitting in the middle. There was no furniture. The hard mud walls were high and windowless, smooth and neat. A soft, pale light suffused the room through an opening in the reed and palm-bark ceiling.

His grandfather was very slender. His costly black Kashmiri robe hung from his sharp shoulders over a cotton waistcoat, with mother-of-pearl buttons showing underneath, and his face was frightful. One eye was a lusterless white, like a stone or the bead of a cheap necklace, the other reddened and squashed, with a deformed eyelid. His lower jaw was broken and crooked, and because of it, Grandfather spoke with difficulty; he generally avoided speaking at all. But under his beautiful, majestic turban he had a noble forehead that filled his grandson's heart with love. Before his grandfather stood an inlaid wooden bookstand where a large book always lay, upon which his grandfather set his palms, or what were left of his palms. Indeed, he was missing all the fingers on his hands, but what remained of them was graceful, so much so that one might easily have imagined that this was how hands ought to be. The grandson sat in front of him without drawing near, and Grandfather did not break his silence. The grandson contemplated him for a long time and wondered what was left of Grandfather, now that he lacked his eyes, hands, and tongue. Then he wondered, with the same earnestness, what his grandfather really lacked, if he was still a beloved person.

His grandfather lived in this house by himself. The house was located in the exact center of the town: every alley led to it. It was the largest house, and more splendid and stately than any other. Even so, it was made from the houses, from the people's awareness of an intensely obscure and mysterious area. The journey here was arduous. If one were to ask about it, the answer would be slow in coming, or there would be silence. But one could discern the prevalent certainty that the grandfather was old, and the descendants scattered through all the houses in the town traced their lineage to him. It was a troubled certainty but predestined, which had to be endured and followed.

The grandson was passionately but secretly fond of his grandfather and never bothered him with confidences or chatter, though his silence could not hide his secret from uneasy eyes and anxious hearts. It was his distinguishing feature, and people watched him with doubting looks and fear. But there was no release; if there was a moment of silence, and the cauldrons of hatred boiled, and the area of ruin spread, then a journey to his grandfather's was predestined. The grandson went into his room and sat before him, remaining there in silence for a long time. Then he began to play, sing, or turn somersaults. He enjoyed profound and genuine safety and could take pleasure in being himself.

His grandfather's servant was a tiny, wizened old woman who always stayed in a small, dark inner room. Though the grandson saw a great deal of her, he never spoke to her, nor did he even know how his grandfather summoned her to come to him. He did not call out for her; when a cloud of displeasure settled over his face, there she was. She took off her sandals at the threshold and walked over the matting to where his grandfather sat and squatted before him, looking into his face. She knew what he wanted without his speaking a word; it was always a book that she brought him, opened to the page he wanted, and set out before him. She would then take the other book and put it away, while his grandson marveled at how all this went on without a word being spoken.

This led him to think that there was a sense beyond the senses; perhaps it was the most intense speech, and the most utterly eloquent. He loved his grandfather deeply, but his love did not distract him from play or study, though he had read all his grandfather's books and thoroughly learned the wisdom and knowledge in them; perhaps this was the continuity between them. Perhaps he sensed his grandfather at night, when he was sleeping, between the love of his mother and father. He would arise at the whispered call, put on his shoes, walk through the neighborhood to the gate, open it, and go in to his grandfather. He squatted before him and knew what he wanted. It was up to him, then, if he wanted that link, to train himself to love his grandfather, to read his books, to read the lessons and memorize them.

But what was the connection between this woman and his grandfather? She was his relative, one way or another. Perhaps she was the daughter of one of his uncles who had died long ago. No one told him about the woman's kinship to his grandfather, perhaps because it was not important. The way to his grandfather was not through kinship but through love and reading. How had he not known this fact, when it was close enough for his nose to bump against it? Reading and love. Love and reading. But was it a long road, as long as a whole lifetime, and did it yield nothing until old age? The grandson laughed, imagining himself old and shriveled, coming to the inner room, to his grandfather's alarm, slipping off his shoes at the threshold, and advancing across the mats to squat before the book holder. He laughed hard and flopped over where he lay in bed.

If he saw that his grandfather was absorbed in reading and wholly engrossed in it to the exclusion of all else, he stole over to the bookcase in the next room. The silence, smell of earth, and sense of transformation made him dizzy. The walls were covered with rows of books, from the floor to the ceiling; light fell on the leather spines from a window set in the ceiling. Reed mats were spread out on the floor, in the middle of which stood a low table with various papers, an inkwell, a quill, a box of white blotting powder, and a large, bronze cylinder.

The grandson handled the volumes, one by one. He flipped through one for a while, then put it down and picked up another. Its quantity of letters, words, idioms, and constructions did not help him to read, but even so, he resumed turning the pages and contemplating them. The rivers of print came from no one knew where and moved onward, never to return, in even rows all the way down. Did they appoint the Fates and assign natural law to the world, or were they the moral formulated after remorse? Whatever they were, they were neatly arranged.

While not reading, he was engrossed in contemplating the letters and the archaic style of the script. The wasteland of the Koran school had taught him otherwise. If the letter *mim* was elongated, he added an *alif* to it. The grandson did not understand that this was ungrammatical. The elongated letter *mim* was ringed only by the *mim,* and the writer hàd to indicate that with a long-A stroke over the *mim*. As to the one with an *alif* added, this was something new, the pivot of two neighboring letters. The grandson was displeased by the style of the script in the Koran school, so he took over his grandfather's books, where the letters were adorned with signs for every meaning. He also loved the illustrations in the books. They were nothing like people; or people, more precisely, were nothing like them. The moral of the pictures was, in any case, wise and sad.

If the grandson did not grow tired, he sat at the low table

on the matting and reached for the bronze cylinder. It was large and heavy. He opened it and withdrew a scroll of paper, spread it out, and began to read. It was the history of their family. This land had once been wild, open country, echoing with the roars of lions. Then Sidi Qutb, the head of this family, arrived; his tomb stood in the cemetery outside of town. His wife came with him. She was the daughter of Sidi Hasan al-Din, who was buried in the neighboring village. In this wild country Sidi Qutb built a house, begat children, sowed the land, and filled the world with goodness and prosperity. The grandson was delighted every time he read these details, for he was the scion of this Qutb—a copy of him. He rolled out the wrappings of the paper and read.

And then he begat, and begat, and begat. So-and-so betrothed So-and-so and begat, and begat, and begat. So it went, for endless lines and uncounted names. They were all of the Qutb family, and all had died, and now they were all buried in the village cemetery. He thought as he contemplated the names written in his grandfather's strange script. He embellished every name in the scroll with some vision of the person living and roaming the earth. The scroll was another, pulsating life. The grandson was preoccupied with the question that engrossed him every time: Where was the truth? The world of the tree, with its trunk, branches, leaves, buds, blossoms, and fruit, was faced with another, buried world, from the roots that spread out tapering down to roots as fine as hair. They say the tree's buried world is bigger than its visible world, and that was its portent. Where was the truth?

It must cover both worlds, with each world being one half of the other. The Qutb family was truly half-buried and half-visible. Life is half the truth, and the other half is death. Then his heart skipped a beat from what he knew of the life of the Qutb family. From barrenness and ruin in the open spaces and alleys, the houses and the fields, hearts and souls, in hands and in facial features. Was it a multifarious pest of this life over the world of death? The grandson grew dizzy at the ruinous thought. He gazed at his grandfather's face from where he sat on the matting and saw a dull gray cloud knit his features into a scowl.

He saw as if the visible world were given to the slow rhythm of a choir's chant and a mass of weeping mourners, as if the melodious rhythm of every prayer and supplication and cry that ever was or would be came from here. From here it spread and diffused to every house, violently entering the breast of every man, tearfully entering the breast of every woman. The silence in the grandson's heart deepened as he waited for a cry proclaiming a death to split the sky.

Prayer, weeping, and reading. Kind words in the hearts of the wise and knowing. Brown words on yellow pages. Lines of words coming from the earliest time. Anthems resounding on the farthest horizon, shriveled in the roots of time without exhaustion, so that hearts would respond with echoes, so that there would be no failure, only life and death. At this moment all of space responded with a cry of lamentation proclaiming the awaited news.

The grandson said to himself that now his grandfather would have to write a new name in the scroll. But how could the old man write with those hands? Should he dictate to the old woman who served him and have her do the writing? No. The script in the scroll was undoubtedly that of his grandfather. Could the name of the deceased be entered in the scroll of death? Now the grandson had to leave. He took his sandals and rose. When the panel of the huge door closed behind him, he turned back to it. The beautiful knocker amid the majestic gloominess seemed to call upon yesterday to come back again, and whenever the grandson left through this door, he was confident of coming back again.

Death filled the town. Women's cries scourged the listeners' hearts with terror and anguish. People's faces were dusty. The men dazedly repeated the formula, "There is no power or strength save in God." The women's pockets were torn, their cheeks bruised, and their foreheads bound in black headcloths. Everyone was running toward the funeral. The grandson knew all this; he had seen it so many times in his life.

Now he wanted to visit the wife of the deceased. He had loved her for years, and for years had been used to seeing her. She had a room on the flat roof, small and solitary under the weight of the sun. If you were to put a marker on top, it would look like a tomb. He pushed the door and entered, closing it behind him. After his eyes grew accustomed to the darkness, he saw her in a corner of her room, busy doing something. He squatted opposite her and said nothing. He might think of something to say to her, or he might not, but she always had plenty of stories to tell. She murmured a flow of words, monotonous and sporadic, in a voice choked with tears. It broke the spell of the old door and welcomed him into a peaceable and tender world.

She spoke as if she did not intend for him to understand. He watched her lovely brown face and her dark brown eyes, her arched eyebrows and her pearl-white teeth. He watched her solemnly and understood every word; not one word made it past him. At times she saw that he understood and took one of his hands in hers. Once he felt the warmth of her hands around his face. He never forgot that one time and could still feel the warmth on his cheeks.

He visited her often. He pushed the door open and closed it behind him and, after a few moments of squinting, saw her. One time he found her naked, sitting on a little stool in the tub, scrubbing herself. He looked at her. She hesitated a little and then said, "All right, sit down." He sat opposite her and she went on bathing. Every now and then she stopped pouring water so that his loud laughter would not drown out her voice as she talked. She continued to speak as the drops of water streamed like tears down her body. He loved her body. The bath brought out a ripe, rosy tint in her brownness as she carefully and lovingly bathed. When she was through, she dried herself slowly. The grandson said to himself that woman was a noble being. She noticed the love in his eyes—perhaps—and began to speak again until her face was wet with tears, which she dried, then put on a light wrap and got up to comb her hair.

That was years ago. In these later years, the woman gradually distanced herself from him, until he grew to hate the fact that with the passage of time he was getting older, and he did not understand. When he realized that she had no excuse for that, he did not ask her but obeyed her. He kept visiting her, however. He wished to visit her now in her room on the roof, like a tomb in the blaze of the sun, and like a tomb in its interior darkness. A green fly from the cemetery was always buzzing around the room.

The grandson walked toward the sound of mourning and holy recitation. There was a crowd before the door of the house of the deceased, in lines along the walls, squatting and murmuring the Sura of the Eternal.* The mourners occupied the middle of the house; the reciters were gathered in the male reception area, sewing the shroud. But the grandson went up the stairs to the room on the roof, where the deceased was covered with a white sheet and surrounded by rings of women dressed in black, all the way to the walls. A heap of shoes lay on the threshold. He found a spot and sat down silently. The hired mourner's head was bowed and covered with a veil. Her voice was soft but heartfelt, pausing after every phrase for the women to cry out, to go back again to the crying lines.

The silk of the mourning clothes, the warmth of the bodies pressing against one another, the hot tears and wet cheeks, the crying and the rumble of the Sura of the Eternal coming from the street—was this the teary life engendered by the white-wrapped death in the middle of the room? There was a kinship between the momentum of this life at

*Koran 112, also known as the Sura of Unity.

this moment and that of the books in his grandfather's house. There the recitation, lamentation, and the knowledge of death were silent and dusty; hot, pulsating, and damp. The grandson grew dizzy at the ruinous thought. He yearned for the woman, the dead man's wife. She sat weeping at the head of the corpse, shouting and wailing, but he heard in the depths of these sounds the same captivating melody that he always heard in her stories and conversations. He listened to her with all his being, wishing that she could cry or speak forever.

But he had to get up. He went down the stairs to the middle of the house and leaned against the room where the reciters were sewing the shroud. They were more damaged than the people of the town, and sicker. They carried more death than life in their bodies. Thus they were reckless and bold. Perhaps this clergyman had marked them down for the death they had courted by reading, and which they sensed without fear, perhaps gladly. They were the grandson's instructors in the Koran school, to whom he had to listen and understand. He took off his sandals and sat on the reed mat. Beside him was the basket containing everything that had been bought for the deceased's last goods: silken fabric, white and green cotton, silk, and velvet, a delicate bath sponge, fine soap from Nablus, and a flask of perfume. He explored the contents of the basket with his hand, and pleasure rippled through his body. The reciters were sewing and chanting the Sura of Yasin.* Each recited a verse he had

*Yasin is the thirty-sixth sura, or chapter, of the Koran and is traditionally recited in times of adversity, illness, and death.

memorized, and the next man recited the next verse. Their voices mingled as successive verses of the single sura were read, and as the grandson was in the circle, his turn came too. He read: "It was but one shout, and lo! they were extinct." He could tell that his own voice was strong and its tone beautiful. They would repeat the sura until the sewing of the shroud was complete.

The grandson got up and left, going all the way down the street to the desert. The sounds of mourning and recitation receded behind him. He said to himself it had been an exercise in the garden of death, nightmarish and delightful. He wanted to laugh, to lose himself in laughter, to skip and do somersaults. That would be the best thing at his grandfather's. He walked along the road to the cemetery where the tomb of Sidi Qutb was located. Each footstep brought him closer to the tomb. Around him were fields of mud grave markers in even rows. This, too, was a scroll, written with bulky tombs and gravestones on a page of earth. Here in Sidi Qutb's fold were the dead descendants, just as in his grandfather's fold, in the village, were the living descendants. Al-Qutb's tomb had the same reverential aura as his grandfather's house. The grandson stooped where he was and went no farther. He wondered whether al-Qutb was now resting in his tomb with a deformed face, his hands and fingers useless. Did he know the name of every child?

The grandson's eyes scanned the rows of tombs. He glanced now at the village, now at the cemetery. Here was the abode of those who had died; there was the abode of those who had not yet died. The tombs here were made from the houses there. The lonely silence that ruled here was made of the loneliness that resounded in the minds of the living, of the emptiness in their souls, of the anxiety that turned their eyes to stone in their sockets, paralyzed their hands, and throttled their hearts so that they could no longer feel joy. What was this terrible fate that twisted the hands of his grandfather and Sidi Qutb? Winds rushed through the vastness of time past the tops of the headstones and the roofs of the houses. The noonday sun reigned over the mud markers so that neither the walls of the houses nor the walls of the tombs had any shadow. Twin villages, in the short distance between which people proceeded dizzily, trying patiently to become habituated to their blindness with the sacrament of recitation.

Now the messengers came, men who had hitched their robes clear of their legs and carried mattocks on their shoulders, advancing, preoccupied but determined. The grandson followed them. He sat atop a tomb among the cacti to watch them. They dug and dug, startling the beetles and earthworms. But the mattocks worked steadily, until the hole was as deep as a man's height. Here was the wall. They began to take bricks from it, one by one, until the opening leading to the floor of the grave was round, emitting a strong smell and the flies frightened by the light.

The messengers froze as they stood before the dark opening, amazed. They were up to their heads in the hole. They craned their necks, looking up and around for the gravedigger. He watched them from where he stood. Behind his crude, scowling features was a smile visible only as

light is visible from behind a blindfold. The grandson wondered meditatively why the gravedigger, of all people, was
able to accompany the departed on his journey farther than
anyone else. The question nagged at him as he watched the
gravedigger, seeing nothing but the mysterious smile behind
his crude features.

Now the gravedigger took off his shoes and placed them
side by side deliberately at the edge of the hole. He stretched
out his hand to the messengers, who held onto him until he
was lowered firmly to the bottom. Squatting, he moved into
the pit of the grave, bare feet first. The messengers handed
him a bowl of dry earth. Now he was making a smooth, dry
bed for the expected deceased.

*N*ow, from afar, the rumble of the mourning throng's recitation and footsteps could be heard. It was mingled with the
group of women's shouts, which deepened the majesty and
dignity of the recitation. The grave was open and listening as
no ear had ever listened. The gate to the afterlife. Now the
gravedigger waited in the darkened vault. It was an intensely
low and strange moment. The grandson imagined that the
body of the grave was a beating heart that felt sorrow, a heart
that would continue to pound until the cover was lifted from
the bier and hands appeared to deliver the corpse into the
darkened opening.

When that happened, silence fell, with only the sound of
the noonday sun beating down on the crowns of the men's
heads, under their red sheep's-wool skullcaps, as they stood

observing. A professional reciter slipped out of the silent throng and walked to the far side of the grave, where he stood humbly, shielding his head from the sun with a handkerchief, as if using it to focus his speech to the occupant of the new grave. The gravedigger came out and piled in the dirt until the pit was full. He patched up the hole between death and life. It was a moment of understanding, wisdom, and relief from fear, even if the face of the earth did bear a scar.

Everyone moved away in the direction of the village, and the cemetery was solitary in the silence. The grandson was still squatting on the tomb. The sun beat down pitilessly on his skull. He watched the backs and the heads of the departing people. He was dizzy and depressed. Perhaps they knew he had stayed behind, watching him cautiously and suspecting something. Was he dreaming, or running away from a fever? Was what he saw real? Was this the feminine hand holding a little iron ball on his grandfather's door? Was the sun making him see things, or was this real? He felt the dark and damp of his grandfather's room. He saw his grandfather. He sat before him, his eyes and heart full of tears.

The journey here today was not arduous, and those voices poisoned with rancor and hatred did not sound from deep within the houses. The women gathered, heart to heart, sorrow to sorrow, wearing black, with bruised cheeks, shedding hot tears over the deceased. The wife of the deceased stood up. She came and sat before her husband's grave to accustom him to his first night of solitude. She was gentle and sweet. She saw the grandson and took his face in her hands. He felt their heat, and his tears ran over her fingers.

THE GRAVE

$\mathcal{A}$ dark, damp, putrid hollow, in which flies buzzed and his heart heard the creeping of the mysterious vermin in their lairs and crevasses. The gravedigger squatted on his heels in the shadows and, from this position, moved cautiously. He breathed regularly, and his palms palpated the earth around him until they came upon bones to which clots of flesh and the remnants of a shroud still clung. The gravedigger set the bones aside gently to clear a space for the new corpse. He set them aside gently and deliberately; these were the bones of a man he knew, who lived next door to him all his life. They had been friendly, and they had quarreled; then the man died, and he buried him with his own hands. When he heard about today's deceased, he knew that the man would be buried in this grave, and the old neighbor would have to be pushed aside a little to make room for the fresh corpse. He must, the gravedigger said to himself; yes, we will see him today after long absence. One did miss people, after all, regardless of whether their company had been soothing or irritating. He tossed the bones aside gently, as if he had caught the scent of his old neighbor and gotten a response from afar.

The gravedigger chuckled softly from the pit of the grave. He said, "The corpse is speaking consolingly; now you are going to have a decent man lying beside you. He will tell you the good news of the world; at the least that will entertain you, I know, and at most it will make you angry, because you are a man with little patience for the follies of people." He laughed again, feebly. With his palms he smoothed a resting place for the newly deceased. He said, talking to himself, "We must not leave a single stone to bother him until Resurrection Day."

The gravedigger turned where he sat, took the corpse from the opening, and carried it in his arms to where he laid it out gently in the place he had made smooth with his hands. The feet were pointed toward Mecca, the palms of his hands against his chest. He opened the stitchery of the shroud. Yes. The stomach would immediately inflate and the limbs would swell up, straining the shroud; this would be a torment he must spare the deceased. This was the other death. With his death, a piece of his friends' world was now missing; it was the same whether the piece had been wonderful or miserable; its absence was painful. Yes, one offered condolences or received condolences, walked in funeral processions, and buried the dead, so that a trip to the grave would not be followed with the hardship of return. He squatted at the dead man's feet, praying. When he finished reciting he remained silent, then said to himself: "There is no escape from this end; there is no repeal of the weariness that is our fate."

The gravedigger sealed up the grave opening with bricks, one on top of another. The pit of the grave grew darker with every brick, and the weak glow gradually disappeared. At that point the dead man pulsated with a vague, groping awareness of his surroundings. The voice of the clerical prompter★ came to him instructing him how to answer the questions of the two Angels of Death. "O servant of God, O son of God's community, God has taken you unto Him." So this was death. The prompter's voice went on: "O servant of God, the world has left you, and you are in one of the intervals of the afterlife." The dead man's eyes were two lifeless lumps of jelly, whose lids neither moved nor opened, and yet he could see. He looked into this interval of the afterlife.

The tomb and the vault curved over him. The damp bricks and the wet black layers piled against them. Between the bricks, in their burrows, insects and vermin alerted by the smell of the newly deceased, their antennae twitching, prepared for their exploratory journey, which boded well to satisfy their appetites. Then he sensed that the pit of the grave was redolent of blind flies with acute hearing, guided

★This divine, the *mulaqqin,* is a Koranic scholar who instructs the newly interred Muslim deceased what to tell the Angels of Death.

by their ears. The earth around him was moist, larded with stones and the remnants of bones. He saw the rags of the dead who had preceded him. The black cloth of the shrouds, fragments of skulls, and skeletons were still stained with rotten or dried flesh. He knew the people. What encounter was this, in which wonder and silence reigned? The prompter's voice was gone, and he was not long troubled by its absence.

He was troubled by pains that were starting in his stomach, chest, head, arms, and legs. Pains in every cell and vein of his being. The pain worsened until it became a torment that left its marks on his outstretched body. His corpse inflated until the shroud wrappings nearly came undone. His face swelled and turned black, its eyes became lusterless, and its features lost their shape. His tongue and lips rotted. His orifices dried up, and the pit was filled with a vile smell. The flies in the tomb stirred in agitation. The body decayed. The wonderful system of cells that had lost its life in his flesh, fat, and glands, in his heart, brain, liver, and lungs, collapsed. The veins, sinews, nerves, and tendons ripped apart. Worms as delicate and slender as needle shafts emerged from cocoons and began to munch the rotting bowels.

So this is death. Is it not a scandal that he cannot scream? Nor can he turn away or get up, but he can see. He sees his face wearing the ugly mask of death. Behind that he can see his face in all its purity and its radiant beauty. A glance like the one that shone in the face of a knowing clergyman who was asked about him; he saw the questioner's unease, beset with worry, and he gazed at him with a face in which shone the beauty of knowledge. The dead man knew this beautiful look; it attracted him. Now he saw it in his face. He was neither surprised nor happy but assailed by a profound certainty that this was the real thing, and the others had just been samples.

So this is death. Isn't the essence of it overwhelming? It freed the being from the bodily element and thus achieved liberation from want: what the body demanded and what was demanded of it. The need and the needed vanished, ugliness was banished, and the power of vision shone. This vision was not like the kind effected by the gaze falling on something seen, revealing what is facing it, but the total perception of the thing seen, its appearance and its secrets, in its movement or stillness according to the laws of its existence without prompting or impediment, a vision that grew more pure, distinct, and all-encompassing the more completely it freed the being from the body matter.

At that time his whole life on the surface of the world came to him, everything, what had changed and what still remained, every time, what had passed and what was left. Every person, those who were dead and those who were still living. It all came to him absolutely, without coercion, untimeliness, or violation of order. It did not surprise or delight him, kindle malicious joy, regret, or resentment; it was only knowledge.

He saw the night in their village, lit by brilliant stars, like a canopy over the houses sheltering the slumber of people and the silence of things. He saw his mother lying with his grandmother in his uncle's house. He saw her at one of those hours of the night in which deep thought deprived her of sleep. Her husband had had a difference of opinion with her brother and the dispute had blown up into an argument, which turned into a fierce fight and, now, a feud that could not be patched up. People knew that a sister had to take her brother's side in a dispute with her husband, no matter whether he was right or wrong, and so that is what she did. She left for her brother's house, leaving behind the husband whose fetus was inside her and with whom she had spent the happiest days of her life.

His mother had a gentle face and delicate hands. She was twenty years old when she married her twenty-four-year-old husband. She had been able to satisfy her young man's feelings of early manhood: before all others, she was an obedient wife who honored him, and among them, she was a kind mother and loyal sister. At night she gave him personal pleasure, offering him her tender body and her thirsty soul. People swore that the marriage was a success. The marriage was blessed a third time when she had her husband's fetus in her belly. Then came the dispute. The pregnant woman ran from her husband's house to her brother's house and back, crazed with fear and despair, trying to mediate between the two sides before they grew so far apart that there would be no hope of reconciliation. It was no use.

At that time the dead man had been a dribble of sperm taking form in his mother's belly as she lay beside his grandmother in the room in his uncle's house. He saw her prostrate body. He saw her heart's troubles and her insomniac soul and the failure of her mind. He saw the blood in her veins, the secretions in her glands, the components of her bodily fluids, and her nervous system. The poison of fear and sorrow circulated through the ruined body on the bed until it disrupted and perverted all its vital functions.

At the same time, his mother's brother lay in his room beside his wife, inwardly burning with hatred for his sister's husband and his cousin. He cared little that he would die; his sister would not be his enemy's recreation by night or his servant by day. At the same time, the father lay in his room alone, beside his wife's empty bed, upon which he gazed, torn apart with pain, but for him, death would be preferable to apologizing to his cousin and setting his mind at rest by hearing of his pregnant wife's return to his house. The night closed over him, and over the grandmother, who was sharing her daughter's torment and finding no answers. They were all waiting for the baby they would swaddle in his mother's shawl, waiting for a cause to be born with an effect that deformed his fate until he died.

Now the dead man knew that his mother's brother had loved him and hoped to adopt him as a son, for he had only one daughter, after whom he desired no more children. But his uncle saw a resemblance to his father in this nephew and knew that he was his image in any case. He knew this and, blinded by rage, tormented his sister and her son. The child slept beside his mother in the night; he watched her eyes, in which all joy had died, and her body, which withered with every passing day. He saw the state she was in and hated his uncle bitterly, waiting for the day his father would take him and his mother home. But the uncle divorced his sister from her husband with a judge's order. The moment the mother heard the court's decree of divorce, she was struck by tuber-culosis. Within a year, she collapsed before the armies of germs that invaded her lungs, and died.

His mother died, but the child she had carried in her body was weak and terrorized; he carried his father, his uncle, and his grandmother in his body, along with their divisions, the feelings that battered them, and the weakness that shackled them. The child carried his painful legacy and hated every corner of his uncle's house until years later, when the judge asked him if he knew his father and whether he would like to live under his protection. He answered with a shriek of "Yes!" and ran to throw himself into his father's embrace. His father hugged him close. He loved him. He took his son with him when he went out by day, made room for him in the bed, cradled him in his arms, and stayed awake, watching him. The child was delighted with his father, and delighted to leave his uncle's house. Now he knew that his uncle had spent the nights prey to sorrow: his sister and mother had died, his nephew had left, and he had only his ailing daughter and a wife whom he could not help give him another child.

At night, the child felt his father's sleeplessness tainting his happiness with fear. He was anxious about their love for each other and did not know the source of his father's insomnia. Now he knew that his father, who was under thirty, wanted to marry. And did. The dead man saw himself, now, sleeping beside his father on the big brass marriage bed. Through the thin fabric of the curtain he saw a bench beside the bed, upon which lay a cushion and pillows; a carpet on the floor; and, at the far end of the room, a wardrobe with a large mirror. In the morning, however, he found himself sleeping on the bench; his father's wife had taken his place on the bed. At that moment, a never-ending hatred for her broke out like a war in his heart.

Now he saw her lying on the bench beside the bed, sleep eluding her, awaiting in fear the moment her husband would call her to him. She had never loved any man, whether father, brother, or husband. All of them scorned her. She would never have married had she not been forced. Although she was unable to save her body from the humiliation of marriage, she saved her soul from it, giving her husband a cold, unresponsive body—as if it were not hers.

Then his father sent him to the school in the regional capital. He lived with the rest of his father's brothers, in an upper room in an old building. The stairs that led down to the courtyard of the house were dark even in daytime, and there was a well for drawing water and an outhouse in the courtyard. It was always dark, damp, humid, and stinking. He used to believe what he was told, that the courtyard had been built by pagan genies, but now he knew that the dark, the damp, the offensive smells, the breath of the old building and the contraction of his chest intensified the emptiness and made a tremendous impact on his mind. When his mind and nerves were weak, it had a strange effect on him. He knew that now, and knew that he had never escaped from this experience.

At school, the teacher was frightening. For the dead man had been a village boy, shy and nervous, frequently prey to the teacher's cane for reasons he sometimes understood, sometimes not. Finally he decided to run away. He walked the ten miles back to the village, spurred by the anticipation of his passionate sprint into his father's arms, but his father's face darkened with sorrow when he saw his son's unsuccessful return, and he instantly ordered him back. The boy again fled to the village, away from the teacher's tyranny and the ghosts of the house, seeking his father's lost love, but his repeated escapes and disappointments caused this love to be lost forever, though in vain he would always try to recover it.

Having failed at school, he had no other choice than to work in the field. He had no way of conveying to his father that he had not been able to succeed. He went freely to the field every morning, with his father's eyes filled with aversion and sorrow, fixed on his back, and he found them waiting for him when he came back in the evening. He did not know where to flee, except toward this father. He sought shelter in him from his pain but collided with his angry silence and the stubbornness that did not allow him to forgive his son for failing in school.

In the field, he often met his uncle's daughter. Now, he noticed, she was tall and slender, with a clear, pale complexion and luxuriant hair. She smiled at him and invited him to visit his sick uncle. He imagined that this was a sign of her infatuation with him. Something about women's infatuation with him filled him with revulsion. He persisted in refusing her invitation to visit his sick uncle. Now he knew that she had never loved him. She had been speaking on her father's behalf. Every time he insistently refused her mediation, he was increasing her resentment of him, as she watched her father move closer to death with every passing day, longing for a visit from the nephew who had rejected him.

On the evenings of these days, he saw his friends and the villagers in the coffeehouse. All of them were infatuated with a girl from the poor part of town. She was stunningly beautiful, in everyone's opinion, and her speech was gentle and refined. Every young man bragged that she was his. Now he knew. He saw her alone in the heart of the night of his wakefulness, everyone around her deep in sleep. She was dreaming of marrying a rich man's son who would rescue her from this poor district and take her to live in the upper part of the village, where she would have a house, livestock, and children.

But none of the young men knew about her dream, or cared. Everyone tried to win her over, but he was the one who succeeded. The sign was that she gave him her body. Now he saw those evening friends in the coffeehouse; they showed him their admiration and hid their terrible contempt for him. He had won her over with the promise of marriage, then started to snub her. The girl realized that his promise had not been a serious one. Already sensing the presence of the fetus inside her, she fled the village, never to return.

After the girl ran away, he lived with muddled feelings of pride and shame. He drove the animals home from the field at sundown to begin his nightly torment of his father's wife. He insulted her with curses beyond human endurance. She defended herself as determinedly as she could. The father would come along and make them stop, but—and he was the elder—he did not take sides with either of them or really care whether their fight was settled. The dead man saw now that his father was using this arrogance to hide his bitter feeling of defeat by his wife's beautiful body, full of coldness and unresponsiveness before his passionate love.

His father knew a widow in the village and took her as his mistress. This was the greatest insult his wife had ever endured from him. She was deeply hurt and could not stop crying. He was pleased—he gloated over it. Now the dead man could see the obscene triangle: the husband, the wife, and the lover. All three were wronged and miserable. The father was looking for someone to propitiate his manhood, the widow was seeking a way out of the lethal solitude that had followed her husband's death, and the wife was made miserable by abuse, fearful for her home and children. He aimed at her, in her misery, his most heartless insults, out of gloating and revenge. He came to wish the widow the grief of marriage to his father, hoping that she would come to harm.

His father decided to marry him off to the widow's daughter. He was surprised at the decision—he had never even noticed the girl. His father was clearly searching for an excuse for visiting the widow's house without causing gossip. He began to watch his fiancée in everything she did. One time he saw her on the canal bank, lying in the shade of a tree, safe from pedestrians in the repose of a midday nap, wearing only a thin gown. Her body was wonderful, but she awakened no lust in him, only a profound repugnance, he saw now, knowing that it had stayed with him until his very last day with her.

One day he encountered his uncle's daughter and told her that he wanted to visit her father. He said that he wanted to get engaged to her. The girl said that was now impossible; she was engaged to someone else. At the time, he imagined that she was saddened by his belated engagement, but now he knew that she had been made chaste by the image of her father, who died in his house without seeing him, his sister's son; and she hated him as she never hated anyone before because he begrudged his dying uncle even a visit. And he tried to get engaged to her without thinking beforehand of pleasing her by visiting his uncle, even for her sake alone. He did know not all this at the time, however, and continued to harbor a love for his cousin in his heart until the day he died, after his father forced him to marry the widow's daughter.

He saw it now: his wedding night. Her mother and the midwife showed him between her thighs so he could put his finger into her vulva and take her virginity. She let out a dreadful cry that at the time struck him as spoiled and even flirtatious; now he knew that his finger had caused her terrible pain, and at that moment she felt toward him a hatred that would last until the day of his death. He was disgusted by her vehement passion. He had a low opinion of her. Now he knew that she had never known any man but him in all her life, though she loved only their little boy; she talked to him, and him to her, for hours on end. He spent these long hours grieving about his cousin, whom he had resolved never to see again; and he held to this promise for as long as he lived. Now he knew that she had loved her husband and had been content with her children.

But her image was confined in the house of a husband she did not love, cut off from her love for him: this was the image that filled his soul the night he first went in to his own wife. After her mother and the midwife left with the blood-stained handkerchief, she collapsed on the bed, miserable and defeated, and he left for the coffeehouse. His friends were astonished to see a bridegroom abandoning his bride on their wedding night. They marveled at his capacity for self-control and his respect for women. He savored their admiration in silence. Now he knew that his wife would suffer for long years afterward from the shame of that night.

He lived with his wife in discord and bitter hatred as he aged toward senility. He decided to become independent of his father, in his home, income, land, and livestock. Now he knew that his father was alarmed by this decision and badly frightened of the decline of his farming with his son forsaking his protection, though he kept silent, saying nothing. At the time, he knew that his departure might devastate his elderly father. He knew this and pressed the old man to acknowledge him, his manhood, and the need for his existence, but his father would not. His collapse lasted from one day to the next, until he died without having lost the hatred that appeared in his eyes whenever he saw his son coming.

After his father died, he felt inadequate, as if he were dying within—as if his body were withering. A tetter spread over his skin. The physiology of his intestines, kidneys, and brain deteriorated. He was deeply attached to his only daughter. He began to be drawn into a state of piety; he stayed in the mosque for long hours, immersed in prayer, neglecting his farm, house, and living. In the evenings, he visited the dervishes' Sufi ceremonies,★ where he prayed until he passed out and chanted God's name until seized by a nearly epileptic state, eating the dirt on the ground. He deteriorated with every passing day, until he found the repose of his grave.

Now he knew what he had not known then, and knew and understood everything, though he did not rejoice at his knowledge; nor did his understanding give him a feeling of superiority. He was not resentful at what had been; nor did any of it please him; nor did he sorrow at his loss. He just knew. He was different from him who had not known, who had been tormented with the annoyance of love, the hindrance of hatred, and plagued by terror. He had lived his whole life consumed by fear of an encircling, imminent danger, whose true nature he never understood, though he felt it coming nearer and menacing him, suffocating him no matter which way he turned. Now his fears were tamed, becoming profoundly calm and secure as they subsided, as profound as death. This was death.

He came into the world ugly and powerless. The world was unable to make him ill, pay attention to him, and spare him from suffering or and doing harm; it only made his inferiority more bitter, with the result that he alternated between the violence of love and the violence of hatred. They were two affections with a single essence: fear. They were, in

★A *dhikr* is a Sufi ceremony involving the repetition of the name and epithets of God.

truth, a single, stormy irritation with a fickle direction, but never altruism, egoism, or respect.

Now he understood, and his being rejected the torment; indeed, it became a part of a greater whole, where his familiarity with all its parts came into balance, and his knowledge was divided equally over all its intricacies. It was a familiarity not stained by the shadow of secrecy, ignorance, or inadequacy, those shadows that are the refuge of curiosity, doubt, suspicion, and confusion, generating unease, apprehension, and fear. It was a familiarity that arose not from the vision that is the struggle with weakness but from the extinction of weakness and the occurrence of death.

Now every image of life vanished from his body, even the nuclei of the cells in the tissues of his organs and intestines. Thus his pain departed and his serenity became perfect, as if the arch of the vault inverted over the tomb receded little by little, its dimensions and horizons opening up. This happened slowly and smoothly, until the walls of the tomb had fallen back to encompass the entire village cemetery. Now it was one plateau, crowded with the dead.

He knew the people he saw and heard. An immense prolongation of sleep, like the stillness before dawn in the courtyard of a crowded anniversary. There is a state of death and dissolution, and there is a state of presence certain of death. There is continuity like that of the continuity of circles of light from many lamps. Then the horizons extended on every side. An ocean of dawn light, surrounded by a circle of dusk.

They were the dead people he had not seen or heard of. Now the edges collapsed and the horizons spread into an eternity of dawn light, unmatched in beauty even by the dawn of a summer day. He knew that these endless horizons surrounding the world of the living were surrounded by the world of the dead, just as a delightful spring forest is surrounded by a two-tiered halo, one for those who had died and the other for those who have not yet died.

Now knowledge was no longer an added part of his being; his being itself became part of the greater existence and enclosed it. It was in itself knowledge. The vision became an onlooking reality; the longing, a pleasure; the fear, security and repose; and unease, a communion. Let the two angels come from the greater existence. Their pens are dry and their scrolls furled; the event has become an image, the image is elevated to words, and the words are the secret, the keys to the gates and their locks, possessing man until his death. When the angel of God's secret died, the veils were drawn aside, the support fell away, and there was light. And here they come, the two angels.

THE TWO ANGELS

They are two lofty beings, emanating nobility, from whom all innate failings have been banished.* Their faces are radiant, and their heads are thick with hair. Their beards are full, their smiles pleasant, their clothes white; their arms hang obediently down, neither tense nor anxious. They walk barefoot, but their feet carry none of the dust of the earth. When the dead man draws opposite them they greet him.

THE TWO ANGELS

Peace upon you, dead man.

THE DEAD MAN

Peace upon you, angels. I thought Aramaic was the language of the grave.

*Naker and Nakeer (sometimes called Munkar and Nakeer) are the two Angels of Death who question the dead in their graves on matters of faith.

(That is, they may have greeted him but did not actually pronounce words; nor did he hear them produce voices. This was a pleasant, friendly intention the dead man recognized, after a shudder that passed through the angels' soul and spoke gladly to his soul, which was his response to their greeting.)

NAKER

We aren't surprised that you didn't think it might be Latin, for example. What impresses us is the purification of the language of the grave of the ordinary, everyday language.

NAKEER

Language is first born in the emotions, as a vision expressing desires or fears, and descends to the storehouse brain to search its memory for suitable structures. Generally, the structures are less warm and precise. They suffer from distortion, and they fall short when converted into the words and gestures that pass between a speaker and a listener. So the truth is that the language of the grave is the vision of the emotions before it can be subjected to distortion and damage.

THE DEAD MAN

So language is spared the imperfection of the body?

NAKER

Spared also the attribute of judgment and questioning about good and bad deeds.

NAKEER

But as every human act necessarily embraces in itself its motive, man is in a constant state of examining his deeds so as to avert confusion between the deed and the motive for the deed. That is the question.

THE DEAD MAN

By that you mean the intellectual view.

NAKER

The mind is one of the body's faculties. It is affected by weakness, just as they are.

NAKEER

The collective mind also is affected by the times of decay, stupidity, force, and oppression that affect the group.

THE DEAD MAN

You put motive beyond the mind, then.

NAKER

I was not talking about the mind, but the mind of a specific individual in particular human conditions or a certain collective mind in particular human conditions.

NAKEER

And we weren't talking about motive, but the motive of a specific deed in specific circumstances.

THE DEAD MAN

It is the intellectual view in the end.

NAKER

No, meditation—an attempt to understand the true direction of the pulse of the soul as it frees itself from fear, ambition, or lust.

NAKEER

Choosing a deed or the rejection that confirms the existence of the doer and does not endanger his progress confirms the existence of others and does not endanger their progress.

THE DEAD MAN

So judgment is denied, then, and torture is necessarily denied.

NAKER

It is not a question of grasp but of understanding.

NAKEER

In order that the levels of knowledge belonging to the participants in this talk be equal, the condition for your participation in our talk was that you be dead.

THE DEAD MAN

So three people are needed to talk, and I am the third. What is the purpose of the talk?

NAKER

To measure the distance between deed and motive.

THE DEAD MAN

What if the deeds are in conformity with the Law?

NAKER

The Law is one of the things we must examine, dead man.

NAKEER

Thus the rule goes from being a higher model of meditation to being the object of this meditation.

THE DEAD MAN

Then it loses its stability—it loses its imperative power.

NAKER

It gains a new imperative power procured in the world of the rule, which drives instincts—rather than responding to them.

NAKEER

This imperative power does not come from the duty of power but from mankind's wish to conform to a rule. In this way, deeds are distinguished by their doer and object, by the circumstances of the deed, the doer, and the object, not by a higher model of behavior, indisputable and imperative.

NAKER

It is not the most exemplary deed but the most exemplary man.

THE DEAD MAN

So what is the point of judgment?

NAKER

The extent he has been justified, and how he has failed to be justified.

NAKEER

That is, whenever it is a question of man's denial of the voice inside him, or of his not listening to it carefully. That voice, in its pure state, before it is stained by corruption and distorted by circumstances, is the measure of death, which is contained by life.

THE DEAD MAN

Death is an extension of life?

NAKER

Yes, as there is no control of events but a reading of them.

THE DEAD MAN

The search for death under heaps of weakness and the malice of time and of people.

NAKER

And a look at the oppressiveness of the confusion between the deed and its motive.

NAKEER

In an individual's transition from a just man to a man with a role or function.

NAKER

And the ensuing distortion of his instinct.

THE DEAD MAN

Our first job, then, is to look at how we understand instinct.

NAKER

It is the wish of every being to survive and make progress, beginning with the most primitive forms of life.

THE DEAD MAN

It is competition, the condition of one's survival, the killing of another.

NAKER

We must rightly assume that competition is the primitive, malformed form of instinct.

NAKEER

Then instinct starts to reform itself to be at its most perfect in the man who has made his survival and progress the survival and progress of the other.

THE DEAD MAN

Even if the other should be another form of life.

NAKER

Yes, the condition for a man's survival and progress is the survival of other forms of life and their progress.

NAKEER

The primitive nature of nonhuman life forms is no justification for killing or exterminating them.

NAKER

The condemnation of all forms of murder and harm is the essence of all law.

THE DEAD MAN

So law is the expression of nature.

NAKER

In great moments of human history.

NAKEER

When prophecy is the other face of law.

NAKER

So that there was complete harmony between law and instinct.

NAKEER

That is the golden age of every prophecy.

NAKER

Law realizes the genius of human thought, and prophecy achieves the genius of individual man.

THE DEAD MAN

That appears marvelous until it turns terrifying.

NAKEER

It truly is marvelous, until it leads to the cloaking of the Law in sanctity and prophecy in miraculousness, amid the jubilation of the faithful.

THE DEAD MAN

That is a necessary thing, to sanctify texts and faith with miraculousness.

NAKEER

It would be more accurate to say it is a necessity filled with fear, fear of losing the moment of complete harmony between law and instinct, fear of time moving its people more quickly than the Law can move. That is why it stands in the face of this movement with the sacredness of texts and theories of prohibition and torture.

THE DEAD MAN

Otherwise, the Bible would become just another anthology of poetry.

NAKER

It already is, in the hands of a pious slave woman who reads it at night.

NAKEER

Miracles serve to banish the prophet's personality and assign his genius to higher causes. Thus every prophet is the last prophet.

THE DEAD MAN

You do not want to see the news of the prophets and their prophecies in the newspapers and radio bulletins.

NAKER

Why not? That would guarantee that the gates of heaven would remain open.

NAKEER

And then there is the contemplative man, the one who absents himself from the throngs of those who believe in the big theories.

THE DEAD MAN

The idea of throngs and the idea of control are inseparable.

NAKER

Yes, and so the structure of a pyramid is the only thing.

NAKEER

At its summit are the pious worshipers and the priests, the theorizers or the elite, the directors or the custodians.

THE DEAD MAN

Here force is essential, to hold the pyramid together.

NAKEER

Yes, force to the point of oppression.

NAKER

For if a man is not honest, let him be a brick in the structure, let him disappear and behave perfectly.

NAKEER

And so oppression is embodied, at the peak of the pyramid, in an idea, or something which neither is a man nor resembles him.

THE DEAD MAN

Then its rights are divided among the agents and the custodians.

NAKER

Injustice reveals itself, most of the time, at the base of the pyramid.

NAKEER

On children, women, slaves, servants, and rebels, in that order.

THE DEAD MAN

Women and children are generally protected with the greatest care.

NAKEER

That is the trifle they are given so that they may satisfy the father's wish to dominate and the husband's wish for sexual gratification.

NAKER

Injustice must be painful, whether it be hell or expulsion from the Lord's kingdom, or torture, or prison, or exile, descent into poverty or into shame.

THE DEAD MAN

Just as paradise must be wonderful, whether it be heaven or the Lord's kingdom or promised abundance or a life of luxury lived by the rich and the stars, as newspapers imagine it and present it to the people.

NAKER

Dreams, with paradise and injustice, complete the trinity.

NAKEER

The dream, in every prophecy, is a time unlike all the others; its people are unlike all the other people, a time that is past and will never recur. Or it is a time that people must strive to attain. In either case, it is remote, indistinct, and oppressive, and contains within itself the impossibility of attainment.

THE DEAD MAN

It is either a historical truth or a scientific truth.

NAKER

In either case, it cannot be fully attained, neither historically nor scientifically.

NAKEER

Prophecies outlaw any attempt to doubt the historicity of the dream's time or its secularness, so that it will remain obscure.

THE DEAD MAN

In this way, the dream is not inspired but a handicapped power.

NAKER

Yes. In such a way that man is torn between necessity and the difficult necessity of change.

NAKEER

And a man torn between the duty of realizing a dream and the difficulty of realizing it for change is the true exemplar of survival at the base of the pyramid.

THE DEAD MAN

The condition for rising, then, is denial.

NAKEER

Denial is the understanding of one thing, and of its opposite, and denying it. It is not a condition for rising in the pyramid but for standing outside it.

NAKER

Hypocrisy is the third state between faith and denial. *It* is the condition for rising in the pyramid.

NAKEER

Thus authority is in the hands of those most knowledgeable about its law, and the most scornful of it; in the hands of those who turn it from an idea into a holy book.

THE DEAD MAN

Into a power to oppress.

NAKER

In order for my people to have this capability, there must be a special preparation with which to pursue violence against itself, in order to kill its natural instinct.

NAKEER

The group creates temples, schools, and other institutions to constrain the body and soul and turn them into a vessel for images and values.

NAKER

Inasmuch as instinct is as pure as possible when life is in its infancy, its freshest years, when life is at its most vibrant stage of life, then life is at that very moment the object of modification and distortion.

THE DEAD MAN

Baby, child, youth.

NAKEER

When life is at its happiest, though it is very strong, distortion is expected.

THE DEAD MAN

A living being's wish to survive and progress is transformed into the law of the survival of the fittest.

NAKER

That is merely a perpetuation of a course of primitive concepts of life and becomes a justification to kill in any concept, to kill individuals or groups.

NAKEER

Even so, man pursues murder slowly or at one stroke, consciously or unconsciously, with pleasure or with revulsion, against himself or someone else, alone or in a group, becoming, by killing, a hero or a coward. But killing is always a familiar thing, like wind or clouds, and a daily habit, like cigarettes or coffee.

THE DEAD MAN

So that death is the only possible recompense for killing.

NAKER

But they mock the genius of death with recitations, gravestones, tombs, and monuments.

NAKEER

They turn it into an institution to perpetuate their kind and to immortalize things like schools, temples, and holy books.

THE DEAD MAN

At that time the stillness is suffocating, and every man and every group are fixed in their most noble qualities.

NAKER

Here everyone must sum up his death, take it in his hand, and defend it.

NAKEER

That is the basic characteristic in the eras of martyrs, but their stories are written in majestic letters in the holy books. The books are raised in lofty temples of marble and recited aloud in moving melody.

NAKER

Other books that tried to know the dead as they were, and to love them as they were, have been forbidden.

NAKEER

For if there is a holy book, then there must be, in exchange, a forbidden, accursed book. The fact is that there must be an absolute book, to exalt absolutely.

NAKER

But what there is, is the temple, which in the first place is the palace of authority, or the center of the oppression apparatus.

THE DEAD MAN

The elements of haughtiness come from an art denuded of its essence, man's ally, so that it may fill this man's heart with awe and fear, to make him kneel.

NAKER

The whole culture of time, the art of it, is poisoned by the view of man from above.

THE DEAD MAN

So we must have a new law and new prophethood.

NAKER

But since every prophet is always the last one, he must be followed by sultans and kings.

NAKEER

They turn the law into a system of oppression, when it had been a system of thought. The legislative institution was distorted into a legal code, and prophecy was distorted into government.

THE DEAD MAN

Thus it is always a matter of reformulating the individual so that he may become a block in the pyramid and reduce his zeal to be human, sacrificing his zeal to be a form until it will be transformed into a preparedness to kill and be killed, in a terrified flight from true life and true death.

NAKEER

You are forgetting the other side: the splendid and significant side of every prophecy, whose essence is the effort to liberate man.

NAKER

And so man's ability to remain forever engenders prophets and cultivates laws. As long as people are alive, there will appear, in one part of the earth or another, at every moment, a prophet with his miracle and the books of his law. The vitality of the institutions of the divine message, and of prophethood, is the vitality of the rejection of oppression.

THE DEAD MAN

But every prophecy gets distorted.

NAKER

So that another prophecy may be born.

THE DEAD MAN

In a thousand years, in spite of that, the distance between slave and hireling has not widened much. There may be yet more oppression, only under a more acceptable facade.

NAKER

So that prophecy would be the beginning of a world and not the end of one. And the Law would be a source of thought and not a constraint upon it.

THE DEAD MAN

When—since the other face of prophecy is the miracle, and the people produce a prophet and see a miracle and drop down prostrate, for they are believers? And how—since the

Law is contained in a holy book, essential in itself, refuting all books but itself, with people thus either believers or infidels?

NAKEER

The prophet of whom you speak—you neither follow him nor attribute his prophecy to a miracle but to the man's genius for overcoming oppression. The law does not exalt the books but human thought; the Law is not directed at believers but at thinkers.

THE DEAD MAN

This is the power to change the world with the aim of man's survival and success. It looks easy in order to become impossible.

NAKEER

It is terribly difficult, but man can do it.

NAKER

The prophecy may triumph.

THE DEAD MAN

How?

NAKER

The people.

THE DEAD MAN

They have been here forever.

NAKER

And will remain here forever.

NAKEER

They pursue death and life.

NAKER

And uphold death and life.

THE DEAD MAN

How?

NAKER

That is the passage of the grave, judgment, and the two angels.

NAKEER

Putting the institution of death counter to the institution of killing.

NAKER

Every dead man alone possesses his death.

NAKEER

He snatches it from the priest's hand, from the rituals, recitations, and processions, from gravestones, monuments, and tombs.

THE DEAD MAN

How?

NAKER

So that he may possess his death.

NAKEER

To be a picture he draws, not a plan whose details he finds in some holy book. At that point, murder is always a defeat and death is always a victory, a man's achievement and his progress.

THE DEAD MAN

But the noise is so loud that one can hardly hear the voice inside him.

NAKER

No matter how loud the noise gets, he cannot contain the inner voice. Nor can he kill the conscience whose fertility and fruitfulness never diminish for prophets and laws.

THE DEAD MAN

It is very deep.

NAKEER

But the grave, judgment, and angels are there.

THE DEAD MAN

I died, and the vision was what it was and how it was.

NAKER

Now we will judge the distance between every deed and its motive.

NAKEER

How was the motive for the deed substituted for the justification of the deed, with man given the role of perpetuating existing institutions and guarding them from becoming the subject of debate?

NAKER

At all times, there was a voice saying no, even if denying it was painful.

NAKEER

That is man's glory. The search is for the moment when man's humanity is born and his glory minimized.

NAKER

With his life the murder of the self and others.

THE DEAD MAN

Now I see. I see now.

NAKER

That is what we were waiting to hear you say, so we could start the judgment.

$\mathcal{T}$he dead man said "I see," and that results not only in knowledge of people and things but in their constant change over time. If the first knowledge is the disappearance of weakness with the coming of death, then the second is the acquisition of strength with the assimilation of death.

If the first vision freed him from the fury of love and hate, giving him profound rest and security, as profound as death itself, then the entire vision acquainted him with the breadth of love and of hate, and deliverance. He knew the extent of torment and the blessing of mercy and, between them, the bridge of death and the voyage of emancipation.

It is no longer a matter of heaps of bones covered with the remnants of shrouds and stains or pieces of flesh, dry or putrid. It is the formula of "what was" and the original, shaping "what will be." It is no longer a matter of armies of vermin coming out of their holes, or blind flies buzzing in the damp, putrid air of the hollow in droning battle, or of thin, brown-headed worms tirelessly chewing. It is a splendid transformation, beyond the grand, prolonged battle in the field between leaving and returning once again to whence it had left.

So he is no longer surrounded by the world of the dead but by the world of the absolute. They are no longer the people he knew or heard of but absolute people: the people who are him. From every face fell the features that belonged to a certain person at a certain time, which then take on the features of man in time. Man is forever, dead or not yet dead. Fact is ripped from fact without dulling a wheel in the unceasing circle of death and life.

Around him, all horizons pull back into an infinity of dawn light, to whose beauty not even a summer dawn can compare, surrounded by a world of people of the eternal and the temporal abodes. The hereafter and the hereafter. The thing is that they see him, they open their interior to him, so that every being may give truth to the greater existence and be part of it.

The angels' faces gazed down on the dead man. They not only had the luminous purity and charm that is achieved in a flash and shines in the face of a scholar who knows the Koran by heart, is known by what he is asked, sees the questioner's unease and anxiety, maintaining a face in which there is grace and learning; they possessed the radiance in the face of a messenger triumphant with the inspiration of heaven or a prophet bearing alone the misdeeds of every sinner, having become the deed, the outrage, and purification all at once, a man as great as man can be.

So that the judgment may now begin.

*T*HE JUDGMENT

THE DEAD MAN
I am ready for judgment.

NAKER
On our way to you, we reflected upon the moment we see as the start of your judgment, your birth.

NAKEER
Usually, we don't have much difficulty discovering the moment in a child's life when his deeds are in line with his nature.

NAKER
We consider that your birth: the moment when you stood in the Islamic Court answering the judge's question,

whether that was your father, and whether he was honest and devout, and whether you, free of any coercion or force, wanted to live with him, and you spoke up strongly and clearly: Yes.

NAKEER

The strange atmosphere around you, the scowls of the judge, the shouts of the bailiff, the meanness of the guards, the crowds of people, your uncle's fury, your father's and grandfather's alarm—none of that distorted the genuine desire deep inside you. That was a great thing.

THE DEAD MAN

For as long as I was on earth, I never forgot that moment. I always remembered it with a sort of tearful sorrow.

NAKEER

That was natural. We may go back to it again.

NAKER

Let's move on from that day to another that came years afterward: when you decided to run away from the school in the provincial capital and go back to the village.

THE DEAD MAN

That is a huge leap forward over the years. I thought I was going to be asked about every single small detail.

NAKEER

That is one of the common misperceptions of people in the mortal world. The fact is that your day of judgment deals with the major events of your life. What happened between those events are so many small, insignificant, repetitive things.

NAKER

Dead man, you imagined that there were spirits in the old house in the provincial capital, but in spite of that, it was wonderful of you to refuse to stay under threat of fear, and to refuse, as well, to reject the torture methods of that school. They had nothing to do with teaching. They were just supposed to turn children into pliable balls of obedience.

THE DEAD MAN

When I went back to the village, I found my father was furious. He ordered me to go back.

NAKER

Now we want to ask you why you went back.

THE DEAD MAN

I could not go against my father.

NAKEER

You went against your uncle in the Islamic Court, and he had greater authority over you than your father.

THE DEAD MAN

Now I see the moment of my submission to my father's wish and my return to the provincial capital. It might be on account of my father's power, of my bodily weakness, which had just begun to appear, of the custom of time that makes obedience to fathers a duty.

NAKER

As long as a man is alive he is capable of saying no. There is never any justification for a man to deny the voice inside him.

NAKEER

You went back to the school, and the intention to run away again was already in your heart. Even so, with this, the energy was finished, and fragmentation, confusion, and disorder began.

NAKER

There was no glory in the second escape.

NAKEER

It was not a condemnation of life in the provincial city in its school and home halves but a declaration of your inability to stand it any longer. So you threw yourself at your father's feet and gave him the right to decide for you whatever he liked.

NAKER

You ran away again after that, until your father decided to make a peasant out of you.

NAKEER

That was actually the dead man's unspoken decision, which the father sensed and acted on for him.

NAKER

The father sensed his son's wish to imitate him, and the lack of any wish to be anything else. He gave him the ability to humble himself.

THE DEAD MAN

No, he was not that malicious.

NAKER

He was doing his part, as a landowner and a leading citizen of the village, and he will be questioned about it. Right now, it is you we are questioning.

THE DEAD MAN

The whole village loved him, impulsively.

NAKEER

Thousands of the faithful in mosques pray for both the righteous and the sinful.

THE DEAD MAN

The comparison is unfair.

NAKEER

Exaggeration for emphasis.

THE DEAD MAN

My father was not a tyrant.

NAKER

He was the head man in the village system, which was a system of landowners and of day laborers, of people hungry to the point of illness and people overfed to the point of nausea. This system by its very nature produces models for oppression.

THE DEAD MAN

He was the head of this system by virtue of blood relationship more than ownership of farmland. That kinship was his link with the people; they had rights by him, just as he had rights by them.

NAKEER

That blood relationship did not give them the right to better working conditions, but at the same time, it stripped them of all feeling of resentment over their lives, so that they became thrilled with a situation that impoverished and oppressed them.

THE DEAD MAN

He was obligated to help anyone in need.

NAKEER

So that they could remain at subsistence.

THE DEAD MAN

He even helped those who wanted to get out.

NAKEER

To create a conciliatory face for his leadership.

NAKER

That idea did exist inside you, but you did not hearken to it at the time.

NAKEER

You hearkened, instead, to your father reciting his maxims and his proverbs and admonitions in his deep, majestic voice.

THE DEAD MAN

Everyone listened to him.

NAKEER

But you saw him when he was afflicted, when he oppressed you.

THE DEAD MAN

He was kind. He had a soft voice.

NAKEER

It was that soft voice that ordered you to go off to the school, and to go back to it, again and yet again, without his asking himself what you were undergoing at home and in the schoolroom. It was that voice that ordered you to marry the widow's daughter without asking whether this marriage was a good thing for you. And there are many other examples.

NAKER

The important thing is that deep in your heart there was opposition, and you suppressed it, until you decided to make a break with your father's house, land, living, and livestock. Only then did you proclaim your opposition. The battle began only when it was not timely.

NAKEER

Your father came to the conclusion that you were unfit to lead after him, and he thought you responsible for that, without it occurring to him for a single moment that he was responsible because he never once in his life even shook your hand, and so he kept hating you for as long as he lived.

NAKER

He will be questioned about that, but now we are asking why you flinched from saying no from the very first.

THE DEAD MAN

Now I see.

NAKER

Now we move on to the next point: your intense griev-
ance against your father's wife.

THE DEAD MAN

I hated her from the beginning.

NAKER

No, you loved her from the beginning.

NAKEER

You were nine years old when you saw her for the first
time. She was stunningly beautiful, as people in the world
say. There was bitterness and oppression in her eyes, and the
sight of her captivated you. But instead of showing your love
for her, your heart filled with hatred for her, and you began
to irritate her.

THE DEAD MAN

She did not want me to fornicate with my father's wife.

NAKER

Did you know no way of expressing your love for a
woman other than sexual intimacy?

THE DEAD MAN

Was that not the time?

NAKER

The first to feel ruinous times are the people of those times. The question of the tomb is: Why are people silent about ruinous times when their hearts are against them?

NAKEER

If you had meditated deep inside you, you would have seen beauty buried under rotten and decaying traditions.

NAKER

But there are ten thousand ways of expressing hatred, and you annihilated it.

NAKEER

On behalf of your father, whose pride scorned him to harm her in return for her coldness toward him. To prove to him that there was no room for any doubt about the existence of something between you and her. When your father married the widow, who was older and less beautiful than his wife, your oppression of her increased until it became atrocious, yet it would have been easy for you to be kind to her.

NAKER

The distance between your deeds and their motives became a huge chasm. We do not see in what you have undertaken the wish to confirm your existence or further it.

NAKEER

But the attempt to be the distorted part of your father, after you failed to become the excellent part of him in his dignity, grace, and eloquence.

THE DEAD MAN

Now I see. Now I see.

NAKER

Now we move on to your relationship with your uncle's daughter.

THE DEAD MAN

Now I know that she loved me, but I always loved her.

NAKER

The question now is why you refused to visit your sick uncle.

THE DEAD MAN

I hated him for wronging me and my mother.

NAKER

The body lying on that bed was that of sick and broken man, not the man who wronged you. A man who loved you and wanted you as his son. He only had one daughter.

NAKEER

The truth is that in refusing to visit your uncle, your only intention was to insult his daughter.

THE DEAD MAN

At that moment my love for her was born in my heart.

NAKEER

At the moment you knew that your insult, by refusing to visit her father, stung her terribly. You loved her the moment you knew that she had become impossible for you to obtain.

THE DEAD MAN

But I always loved her.

NAKER

Without asking yourself about her feelings.

THE DEAD MAN

At the time, I thought she loved me.

NAKER

We are asking you about that time.

NAKEER

You froze the last image you saw of her, then became infatuated with that image. You lived for years avoiding the sight of her, averting your eyes when you passed by her door;

you were filled with emotion when you saw her husband or one of her children.

NAKER

In this way a woman becomes a thing, as she is turned into the object of one feeling or another or some desire or another. The woman object, the human woman, is not even considered.

NAKEER

She knew what you said about her, and for that she hated you intensely.

THE DEAD MAN

Now I see. Now I see.

NAKER

And so now we will move on to your relationship with the country girl.

THE DEAD MAN

That was my greatest sin.

NAKEER

You are not very remorseful about it.

NAKER

When you had her, if we may use the vocabulary of coffeehouse boys, you had achieved manhood, in the sense of aggression, boorishness, and depravity.

NAKEER

Until the end of your life, you remembered that total pleasure with a regret that you call penitence.

NAKER

The price of that pleasure was a woman who fled and an aborted baby.

THE DEAD MAN

The mistake is that I thought she loved me.

NAKER

You did not test this belief, even when every boy in the coffeehouse claimed the same thing.

NAKEER

Her love was her dream of marrying the son of a rich man. It was a dream that the promising look in the eyes of every village boy aroused in her.

THE DEAD MAN

She gave herself to me because I promised to marry her.

NAKER

The truth is that, deep down, she guessed at your betrayal, but she wanted to end her attachment to a dream that appeared to be, with every approaching day, a delusion.

NAKEER

The end was a moment when you got up from her, disgusted with her, and rushed to wash yourself clean of her bodily fluids.

NAKER

You have never let a woman love you. You won the hatred and contempt of the country girl, and you enjoyed it.

THE DEAD MAN

The people in our neighborhood would not have accepted her baby, so she ran away.

NAKER

They accepted her. What they did not accept was her dream of getting out and making a new life.

THE DEAD MAN

Everyone in poor neighborhoods dreams of a house and an ox.

NAKER

But not at the expense of another poor neighborhood. That is the difference.

THE DEAD MAN

I see. Now I see.

NAKER

Now we will look at your relationship with your wife.

THE DEAD MAN

Yes, now I see the moment. I see my father sitting in the dark of the evening, on the balcony of the guest house, alone and helpless. I approached him. He said that he wanted me to marry. At the time, I was happy, but I did not say anything.

NAKEER

You saw in that his acknowledgment of you. You were happy because he was like you in that with the widow: he was marrying you to her daughter. But marriage and the woman you would marry did not occupy you much.

THE DEAD MAN

She rejected the idea of marriage.

NAKER

Not right away.

THE DEAD MAN

Yes, I see that now. She felt safe with the passing of people in the heat of the nap, and divested herself of her outer garment and slept in a light shift in the shade of a tree by the canal. I saw her naked thighs—they offended and disgusted me. I decided not to marry her.

NAKER

Her powerful womanhood frightened you. You were afraid you would not be able to subdue her. You went away from her, with your heart and your head, to your cousin, the unattainable woman.

NAKEER

Whereas powerful womanhood is a sign of a woman's physical and mental health, and it is fitting that a man rejoice in her.

NAKER

But her situation in your family was an offering to your manhood.

NAKEER

As a prominent member of your family, you had to degrade and subdue your wife. The first object served by degrading and subduing her was the annihilation of her womanhood.

NAKER

In order to be capable of doing this, you had to resist the voice inside you until it was mute.

THE DEAD MAN
None of that was intentional.

NAKER
The dead man is questioned about the deeds performed due to the necessity of his role and social position, even with no intention to do harm, if there is in these deeds anything dangerous to the survival and progress of other people. That is the significance of the questions of the grave.

THE DEAD MAN
The path after that was painful: I know.

NAKER
We will now question you about the wedding night.

THE DEAD MAN
The peasant's blood is only the law of the village.

NAKER
No. It is unknown in the area of enforcement.

THE DEAD MAN
A man knows his wife at home and at work and may have slept with her many times before their marriage, and so no blood will be found on the peasant's sheets on his wedding night. There is nothing to keep them away from each other.

NAKEER

If happiness is abundant on both sides, and there are no legal obstacles, and there is a high degree of openness, then that is a legitimate and valid marriage.

THE DEAD MAN

They do not wait for the religious ceremony.

NAKEER

It is not written; it is not a condition for the marriage to be valid.

NAKER

We consider that deflowering to be the beginning of your marriage.

NAKEER

A bloody beginning, and the course thereafter is intense hatred and unending conflict.

THE DEAD MAN

She had no easy pregnancy. She was very hurt. You know.

NAKEER

The whole neighborhood, the whole male society was behind your tyranny over her. She did not know where to flee. The only way to get you away from her was to hurt you.

THE DEAD MAN

She sinned, too.

NAKER

We will question her about it. Now we are questioning you.

THE DEAD MAN

It was a vicious circle of oppression.

NAKER

There was a voice inside you calling to you to halt that circle.

THE DEAD MAN

How?

NAKEER

By taking your wife's hands in yours just once and asking her what was wrong.

THE DEAD MAN

That would have been far-fetched at that time.

NAKER

Not far, close, closer to you than your own insides.

NAKEER

Your salvation may have lain in that. Perhaps.

NAKER

You would have been capable of doing it once you were old and your relationship was a quieter one.

NAKEER

You preferred to bring your pain to dhikrs and dervishes, with your wife left at home.

NAKER

Until the last moment, you persisted in not acknowledging your wife's presence beside you.

NAKEER

The fact is that from the event of your bodily and intellectual being, and the events you have passed through in your life, you were in urgent need of the woman's love. But as soon as this love came near you, it aroused only terror in you, and you became hostile and aggressive. You made yourself miserable, and you made the women close to you miserable.

THE DEAD MAN

I see. Now I see.

NAKER

Now we will look into your relationship with your daughter.

THE DEAD MAN

I gave her all my love.

NAKER

You stayed close to her. You listened to her fears with your heart, trying to shelter her from her anxieties. You were filled with terror.

THE DEAD MAN

I was so worried about her.

NAKER

Her mother watched your vigil over the girl. She asked you softly to let her play.

THE DEAD MAN

I always wanted her to stay inside the house.

NAKER

You were imprisoning her, and you did not know why. You were afraid for her, and you did not know why. You wanted her to be absent from your thoughts. You could not summon her up. When the girl began to grow, to mature and flourish, you were terrified, and you did not know why.

THE DEAD MAN

Yes.

NAKEER

Even though you suffered from the coercion that befell you.

NAKER

Even though her mother had grown weary and senile; she could not wrest her daughter from the claws of your paternal love.

NAKEER

It left an indelible mark upon her.

THE DEAD MAN

I see. Now I see.

NAKER

Then you began to visit their excellencies the dervishes and their evening litanies.

THE DEAD MAN

I was so full of grief over my father's death.

NAKEER

You were grieving over yourself. Your father was, in the society of your village, the only authority authorized to acknowledge you. You spent your whole life at his feet awaiting this acknowledgment. When he did not do it, you decided to leave the house, to put pressure on him, but too much time had gone by and his decision became final. He died with it. You could not take that blow.

THE DEAD MAN

My physical and mental strength had reached the lowest point.

NAKER

You joined the Sufi path.

THE DEAD MAN

Recitation and litanies of God's name, chanting, tambourines, and visits to our beloved shrines.

NAKER

Freedom from what was written, and determined, and imposed, closing your eyes to the Brotherhood's venial sins. Looking into the self, proving it and attesting to it. Dropping the chains of fear from the followers' resolutions so that they would be able to build an ideal society, whose brilliance would lie in the brilliance of every one of its members.

THE DEAD MAN

That is what I wanted.

NAKER

No. You entered the Sufi path without faith, to flee a reality you could not face. The whole time you were trying to defeat your doubt, but you could not.

THE DEAD MAN

The litany was a tremendous moment of truth.

NAKER

And if this moment did not appear to you to defeat doubt, it was because your brain had been destroyed by the sickness and your will had died, and so the judgment of the tomb was removed from the time that follows.

NAKEER

And opened the gates of death to you.

THE DEAD MAN

I thought it was the path to the torment of the grave.

NAKER

It is actually the path to knowledge.

THE DEAD MAN

Now I see.

*I*t was a long and laborious path, and now he had reached its end. The angels departed, vanishing into the light of daybreak like two silver beams. His material being may have been reduced to dry, pallid bones, but the dead man passed on to the bright horizon, of which he became a part. Experience became knowledge; not knowledge between the covers of a book, for only insignificant books had been written, and of those, only the least significant had been read, about the least significant people and things. As to the knowledge of people, of those who wrote and those who read, of those who did not read and did not write, that was total knowledge, absolute knowledge.

That was because people owned death, the transformation of experience into knowledge. In this way, every death is a victory, and people's life is never as it was before one—anyone—dies. People will keep dying, and will die until the institution of death vanquishes the institution of murder.

These are the dry white bones whose flesh and shroud have been consumed by the earth. The earth will gather these bones to it and preserve them in its breast as a reciter of the Koran preserves the verses of the holy book. They remain there forever. People on top of people on top of people. Each indicates a person and his time. The heart of the earth is a biography without beginning or end; its letters are skulls, and bones are its dots and accents. O, what a fine memory the heart of the earth has!

This boundless horizon of dawn light surrounds this world and the next, the hereafter and the hereafter. It reaches every beaming heart. The dead man has become part of this inspired, boundless horizon, in his good deeds and his bad, in what he did and what he failed to do, because he has lived and died.

RESURRECTION

The grandson opened his eyes. He was still sitting on the mound of the grave under the noonday sun. His head burned with age, his strength was sapped, his sight blurred, and the grief in his heart intensified with the deed having reached its end. The grandson opened his eyes, of which nothing but two blue, red-rimmed circles were visible. He did not know how long he had been sitting here under this sun, but he was dizzy and dim-sighted. Perhaps he had slumbered for a year beside the grave marker and cacti on the mound of the grave, and sleep had shown him strange dreams. He wanted to move his arms and legs, to rise, but he was totally powerless, and his memory was confused. The sun must have struck him on the top of his head; he was dizzy, and every part of him ached. He gathered up his load of papers and books, held them to his chest, and got up, staggering, the visible world slowly coming into focus.

Around him was the field of graves, as familiar to him as a shepherd is familiar with his good, peaceable sheep. He put his books on the mound and went to the canal, where he filled his jug, and then began to walk through the rows of graves. Beside every marker were cacti; this was one of his chores. People said that a fresh, succulent cactus on the mound of a grave spared the deceased from torments. People went back to the village after burying their dead. He carried the water, irrigated the cacti, and contemplated the state of the world. He did not water the cacti to spare the dead the torment of the grave; he did it because it was his passion. He was attached to the cactus plants. Most plants were full of life and silence. There was a mysterious connection between graves and cacti—what it was, he did not know. He carried his burden of unanswered questions and passed on.

Around him was a field of graves, squares of silence, headstones, and pots of cactus; they were all now as luxuriant as hearts harboring delicious secrets. He, too, was delighted. He pressed his load of books to his chest and made up his mind to visit the al-Qutb before leaving. The interior of the tomb was whitened with lime, marred by earthen scratches, and haunted by cobwebs and silence. The tomb over it was draped in tattered bunting and surrounded by a broken-branched hedge. Was it silence, or man's inability to hear? Questions that had no answers. Was this the one visited by Job the Egyptian? Job with the boils, every boil a question.★ Job, who was patient with his boils until he found the blessed fleabane on the bank of the channel of Egypt's Nile. He bathed, and his scourge departed. Al-Qutb was a thread-bare turban, a shabby tomb, and cryptic silence.

Now he must return. He bid peace to al-Qutb and left. He looked at the graves and kept walking. He set out upon the road that led to the village. He carried his books under his arm—books and scraps of paper of every kind. Whenever he saw a piece of paper with writing on it, he picked it up. He gazed at it for a long time before adding it to his bundle. He had been enthralled by the letters of the alphabet ever since he had been a young boy in the Koran school. All this Arabic swelled and grew heavy. He made it a leather cover to protect it from the sweat of his hand. He was patient with his burden, which had never left him since he sought learning at al-Azhar.★

His father wanted him to be a great preacher or sheikh to lead people in prayer in a great mosque. When he was organized in his studies, he read a great deal and sank into deep contemplation. The first year, the sheikhs loved him. Only they pitied him because of all the reading. They advised him to confine himself to the required books and then to try laughing, playing, and mixing with his brothers, otherwise his mind and heart would be impaired by his ceaseless

★The Book of Job 2:7, in the Bible.
★Al-Azhar is a mosque-centered university in Cairo, founded in A.D. 967 by the Fatimid dynasty. It is still the most influential religious university in the Sunni Islamic world.

addiction to reading. He tried that sincerely, but when he went back to their village, that strange hour of silence had befallen the world, and his feet carried him to visit his grandfather. He stood before the door, contemplating it until his heart was filled with gloom. At that point he turned his gaze to the delicate lady's hand clasping the little ball. Grief filled his spirit, and a patient smile spread across his face. He pushed the door open.

He went into his grandfather's room and sat in front of him on the matting. His grandfather's breathing was troubled, and there were tenderness and compassion in the old man's face. A moment of connection hard to describe; then he felt the desire to get up and go to the bookcase. Now he knew how to read. He read until the torment reduced him to tears, sitting on the mat, hunched over, deeply disheartened. The old woman entered and approached, a strange affection in her eyes. She took the book from his hand, gave him another book, and opened to the marked page. He read and read, question led to question, and the torment became an addiction. There was no end.

He listened to his sheikhs at al-Azhar eagerly and assiduously, but when they asked him anything he said, "I don't know." The seekers after wisdom were promoted to higher classes, but he spent those long years sitting on the mats in the classroom, listening to the sheikh seated on the bench, and when he was asked anything, he answered, "I don't know." The sheikh grew fond of him and said to him, "My boy, do you know what two and two is? It is four, my boy." The grandson said, "I did not know, sir. I thought four was something different from two and two." "Oh, my dear boy, this is the beginning of real trouble," said the sheikh. Then the sheikh asked the grandson to write something. The grandson wrote in a firm and beautiful script. The sheikh read critically and saw that he had improperly doubled an unvoweled consonant and drawn a diacritical mark in place of a letter. "My boy, you have made a mistake," the sheikh told him. "I don't know," the grandson replied, "but I find that the letters have beating hearts and wise souls, so I think it proper to invite them to speak—and when I do, I've found that what the letters say is right." "Oh, my dear boy," said the sheikh, "this is the beginning of real trouble." Then the sheikh asked the grandson to recite a passage from the Koran, and the grandson recited it correctly and in a beautiful voice, but went from verse to verse out of sequence. The sheikh called this to his attention, but the grandson went on reading in his own way and said, "Sheikh, I am not reciting from the Koran, but the verses in the order in which they were revealed." The sheikh said to him, "My boy, what we have here is the Koran." "The Prophet never read it," said the grandson. "Oh, my boy, this is the beginning of real trouble," said the sheikh.

The grandson began to forget the times of his classes and did not report to the classrooms. He walked through the halls, confused, carrying his books, his turban askew, his clothes disheveled, and his long outer cloak open. He walked between the rooms, listening, guided by his ears. He heard lessons in jurisprudence, rhetoric, and the fundamentals of law and wished he might take part in chemistry experiments or discussions of legal strategy. When he heard something he liked, he entered. He spread out his cloak and sat on it, though he was so skinny that the floor matting and wooden chairs caused him to ache. He listened distractedly, hearing things other than what was being said, or excitedly watched what he saw, then got up, forgetting his cloak. His robe was too short for his thin legs. The sheikh asked him where he had been, and he told about his experiment: when he did it, what he saw was not the same thing that the others had seen, and what the letters and words told him was not what they told the others. The sheikh then realized that there was no use in trying to bring him to his senses using punishment. There was no getting through to him. "Leave us, my boy," the sheikh told him. "We have nothing for you here. My boy, you are destined for solitude and pain. Take up your fate and go. We wish you mercy."

The grandson closed his eyes, immersed in silence, listening closely to the beating of his heart within him. Then he trained his large honey-colored eyes on the sheikh and said, "You are right, sir. After reading comes the journey, journey and the reading, reading and the journey. They are the two paths to love. I am going back to our village, to my grandfather's house and the resting place of Sidi Qutb, where people come and go, bowed under heavy burdens—a yoke, an ax, or a coffin. You see correctly, sheikh, and I will leave. I will travel tomorrow."

He picked up his books, his cloak flying behind him, his turban coming unraveled, his cheeks covered with light fuzz and brown hair. When he grew tired of walking and was impeded by his cloak, he undid the turban and fastened it around his waist as a belt. His clothes did not reach down to his feet in their shabby sandals, slogging along the road. He did not ask about the route but about people. He greeted people and was delighted to be greeted back. When he came upon a good woman or a generous man, he sat quietly, listened, and heard about the land and the crops, seeds, salvaging the harvest, and fighting pests. He heard about the beasts that were men's companions in their arduous journey, about their muteness and the silent language of their grievances and aches. If one wished to know the world, let him look: it had a inscription concealed in the heart of every wise human. If one wished to know the world, let him look: the knowledge of the world was divided among the hearts of all creatures. The grandson turned his gaze and his heart to the remoteness of time and savored the smell of the winds whispering in the boughs of the trees, tossing in waves over the standing green crops in the fields. He walked from a village to a market to a birthplace. He rose from a bench before a house, to a mat in the arbor of a mosque, to a darkness confined under the dome of a tomb. He did not ask where their village was. He said to himself: If the time has come, the path will take me there. And so it was.

He sat before the door of their house, reciting. When his father saw his eyes he grew frightened. "O father," he said, "I will work for my food and the price of my books. Will you rent to me on those conditions?" He worked by day in the sun, and when his workday was finished, he went to the cemetery, watered the cacti, and collected his thoughts a little, thinking over the state of the world. The cemetery had a certain communicative silence, a silence that led to a meaning confined in the arbor of wise hearts. The silence filled his heart, and he suffered if his day contained any remnant mindful of the mosque. When he was through, he sat in a corner, absorbed in his books. But he suddenly sensed the weakness of words, almost as if they were random black scratches on the surface of the pages.

He rose and made the rounds of meetings with men in the plazas at the top of the alleys. The silence was intense; their heads were bowed, and their hearts were smothered like plucked young birds dying. The women were on the ground floors of the houses in unending strife. Poisoned words from bloody, burning hearts. Hearts harbor oceans of the tar of black hatred. The images of torment in the Meccan verses of the Koran. The images of death in the lamentations. A death without recitation, without prayers or processions. A death without sublimity. A death not derived from life, not growing from it; an inferior form of extinction and nonexistence.

The grandson fled the confinement of the spirit for his grandfather's house. He sat in the library and took the scroll of paper out of the bronze cylinder. He read the names of the dead, then closed his eyes, memorizing the names of the living. His imagination raged with the clamor of two worlds, two oceans with no land separating them. People crossed from here to there until one scarcely knew who was dead and who was alive. The names commingled, and so did their features and heights and movements. His grandfather was filling strange sheets of paper with strange script. A language with the sudden and surprising faculty of speech. The grandson got up and sat across from the old man on the mat and rapped his hand in front of him, monotonous knocks expressing tremendous irritation. He wondered whether, if life became corrupted, the corruption of death entered it too. The question worried him until his body was wracked with terrible pains. He lifted his gaze to his grandfather and saw the expression on his face was sorrowful and melancholy. He got up and walked out of the house, then turned around for a look at the door. The delicate lady's hand clasped the little iron ball. That lovely creation amid a setting of gray melancholy. Yes, said the grandson to himself: he would return.

He was very silent. He was calling to himself. He lived among people, devoted to what none of them cared about. They said that he was either a saint or virtually a devil. The mortal world was divided between these two types, to which the paths of modesty, abstemiousness, and reverence were closed. Let us give him our children and he will teach them. They will learn from him, knowledge if he liked, or strength if he so chose. This pleased the grandson, and he said, "Do it."

When his first student came, he welcomed him warmly. They sat opposite each other, their knees touching and foreheads bumping; the lad took out his pen and paper and looked expectant. But the grandson told him, "Tell me something." "About what?" the child asked. "About yourself and the world," replied the grandson. The boy began to talk, and the grandson listened, breathless, asking for more, asking for details; the boy spoke without a pause as the day waned, from the late morning until the sun began to sink. At that point the boy got up to leave: his eyes were not his eyes, his face not his face, his steps not his steps, and his actions not his actions. When the boy saw his father, he was afraid. When his father asked him what he had learned, the boy told him that he had learned much. "About what?" his father asked. The boy replied that he learned about himself and the world. When his father asked about arithmetic and dictation, the boy answered that he would probably learn those the next day.

The next day there were two boys, and then three, and then there were many, both boys and girls. Their fathers asked about arithmetic and dictation and got strange answers, which they did not know how to take or how to understand, and so they suspected that the children were being taught godlessness. They told their children not to go to him anymore, and the children said that it was no use: "He is one of us and he is in us, and even if we stop going to him, we will still be with him." "We will throw him out of town," their fathers said. The children said that it was no use, since the word had been said, and once the word was said, any word, the world would never be the same as it had been before the word was spoken. Absolutely, their fathers said. They imagined that the fault lay in the fact that they had been forsaken between the grandfather's death and the grandson's arrival. They remained silent, afraid and watchful, though tormented.

The grandson went to his grandfather's house. He sat before him on the mat. The ghost of a smile played around the old man's face, ornamenting it like his noble forehead. The grandson remained silent and pleased. He said to himself that the best kind of communion was a wordless one. He said this and vowed to speak only a little. He went into the library, took a book, and became engrossed in reading. When the clouds grew suffocating, he noticed the old woman coming. She selected a book and put another before him, open to a marked page. It was inevitable that one day he would look into her eyes, and now he did. He saw a strange beauty in her eyes. He kept gazing into them, and she knew and gazed back at him through them. Now he knew the meaning of the word *mother,* the word *sister,* the word *beloved,* the word *confidant,* and the word *companion.* The words were filled with treasures of meaning, treasures in caskets closed with rusty locks. What was knowledge if it did not smash the locks, open the caskets, and salvage the treasures from the depths of the words?

The children slunk through the alleyways, going from door to door. The children crept over the canals and moved from shadow to shadow. Their gait and movement, their faces and eyes. The children toiled under the sun, read in the rooms, lowered their eyes, and recited greetings. The children were there; from where he was he saw and heard them. When they gathered, he sat down until the session was over. He listened to them—they surprised him with what he had not known.

When his father died, he bequeathed him a plot of land.

He said to himself that one ought to know farming and must learn from cultivation and work, austerely and selflessly. When the harvest was good and plentiful, he gathered the children and asked them. They told him, "Don't give anything to the poor. Donate what you have to the mosque as a religious endowment. It is a good place, where people perform ablutions, meet to pray and study, and stand for long periods in thought behind the imam. The mosque is a worthy place. It has been home and school since the earliest times." They told him to donate his land and to buy mats, kerosene, books, and copybooks with the proceeds. That way he would not be a landowner but the mosque's servant, which would be more meritorious and a little more correct for him.

He spent the daytime farming. When he was exhausted, he went to the cemetery to care for the tombs and water the cacti and rested for a little while under the dome of al-Qutb's tomb. He went back to the mosque to sweep and light the lamps; then he retired with his books or went to his grandfather's house. He spent the time in his library. If he grew unhappy, the old woman came and comforted him, giving him the strength to read another book. The grandson asked himself: "Is this why Grandfather lives and doesn't die? Do you see her giving me the love that frees me from illness?"

For he was ill, but he lived with the illness and bore it patiently. He went to the provincial capital, ignoring the filth of the city and the dazzlement of its people and buildings, and sought out its wise sheikhs. He sat at their feet and listened to them, then made the rounds of the bookshops, spending a great deal of time in them, and came home with the books he liked. He was afraid of the doctors who were haughty and claimed to be knowledgeable, and trusted the ones who listened well, whose eyes expressed perplexity and whose foreheads showed weariness and deep thought. At that time he listened to them and bought the medicine they prescribed. He visited the herbalists, browsing among the various kinds, going by the smell, finally taking home many packages of things to boil, soak, cook, and press for juice. At night, he listened carefully to the flow of life through his body, bearing his illness patiently and treating it with drugs and herbs, but it was no use.

The illness swept through his body like the water of a river inundating parched land. He got up from his bed and opened the door of his house. The first rays of light were about to appear in the dewdrops on the tender flower petals. He walked through the alleys, oblivious to his pains. The houses were not houses. The truth is that while they were invisible to the eye, they were not absent from the ear and the heart, if one gave a free hand to his heart and his imagination. His ear was trained and his senses alert. Thought was not thought. In this place in the mortal world, fear agitated his heart every time. Now, no. Was this death, or was his illness making him hallucinate, or was it the fact that poisoned words no longer flowed from within the slumbering hearts inside the heaps of sleeping bodies, words that had broken his uprightness, bowed his head, and spread the illness through his bones? Other words blessed the children. His emotions sharpened. He ran, barefoot, and threw himself down, his arms spread, his palms open, against the gate of his grandfather's house. The cold of the iron nails filled his heart with repose. His fingers moved, groping for the knocker, until he located it, feeling the delicate frozen fingers of its hand. He laughed, and the sweat ran down his feverish body. He pushed the door open and went into his grandfather's room. His grandfather and the old woman were sitting cross-legged on the mats, their knees touching and their faces very close, the lamp keeping vigil. Between them an open book lay on the bookstand. They were both dead.

The grandson joined them. His feverish body shivered, and his sweat and tears streamed down. He looked at the open page and read: " 'Yasin. By the wise Koran, lo, you are one of those sent on a straight path. A revelation of the Mighty, the Merciful, that you may warn a people whose fathers were not warned, so they are heedless.' "★ He kept reading until the light of day filled the room. He extinguished the light and enshrouded the two corpses while clearly reciting, " 'It is We who give life to the dead and record what they have brought before and that which they leave behind. And We have accounted for everything in a clear book.' "

He drew their garments over their legs and placed their hands over their chests. He closed and covered their eyes and placed the bookstand, with the Koran on it, at their heads. He recited aloud in a clear voice to fill the emptiness that had

★Sura of Yasin (Koran 36.1–6, 15).

filled the interior of the house with the death of these two beloved people. He was the orphan whose heart, once stricken, would never be innocent again. The grandson went into the library, reciting. He sat down on the mat by the low table, took the bronze cylinder, and removed the paper scroll. He spread it out before him and commenced to study it. The last word in the last line was *al-Qutb,* and before that was *daughter of Sidi Hasan al-Din.*

The grandson took the old man's quill and dipped it in the inkwell. He added the words *The Grandson* to *al-Qutb* on the last line of the register. He watched the ink glisten, then spread white blotting sand on it and blew it off. He looked at the word, pleased that his script was exactly like his grandfather's. He rolled up the scroll and replaced it in the bronze cylinder.

The grandson returned to his grandfather's room. He sat on the mat, where he used to sit when he was a boy. He closed his eyes and tried to recall the old feeling of trust but could not locate it. Yes. His grandfather was dead. He remembered the children. They were now in the fields or in their homes, in the alleys or the canals, or perhaps in the mosque studying together. The grandson felt exultant and afraid, feelings akin to unease. It was a delight to be a child in the protection of a great father; it was torment to be a father with children. But it was no use. He glanced at the two shrouded corpses and rose. He went from his grandfather's room out into the little courtyard, into the blaze of daylight in the alley. As he walked, he turned back to the door of his grandfather's house. The delicate lady's hand clasped the little ball. He said to himself: What could be more beautiful? He would never come back again. But they would come— other people would come.

He walked through the neighborhood. The sun was intense, and he walked as if he were carrying it on his head. He trembled with fever, as the sweat poured down his body and his eyes streamed with tears, but he never stopped reciting. He longed to see her. He headed toward her house. He had loved her for years. All he could do was love her. For years he had been used to the sight of her. She had a room on the roof, small and solitary under the weight of the sun. He pushed the door open and entered, closing it behind him. She approached him from the corner of her room to welcome him. He sat with her, quiet and listening. She spoke, and he listened longingly. She spoke of her grief and torment, and when she saw that he was listening, and that he understood, she clasped his elderly hands between her own childish, tender hands. Then she rested her soft, gentle cheek lovingly against him; he could still feel its warmth in his hands now.

But today he found her naked, sitting in the washtub on a stool, bathing herself. He looked at her. She hesitated a little, then said, "All right, sit down." He sat opposite her, and she went on bathing. Every now and then she stopped pouring the water so that his loud laughter would not drown out her voice as she talked. She continued to speak as the drops of water streamed like tears down her body. The grandson realized that he would always love her body. The bath highlighted the ripe, rosy tint in her brownness, as she carefully and lovingly bathed. When she was finished, she dried herself unhurriedly. The grandson said to himself that women were graceful and powerful creatures. She noticed the affection in his eyes, and her face became radiant with a smile. She told him that she was free of her husband, she felt her soul was free and liberated, and her heart was now devoted to one of the pretty, broad-shouldered, humpbacked children, who had large eyes and spoke little but, when he did, whispered softly.

She spoke in a monotone, her sweet voice pausing delicately. She spoke, and the grandson contemplated the pleasure in her beautiful face, her brown eyes, her arched eyebrows, and her teeth that were as white as pearls. Now she put on her gown and combed her hair. Now she was like a bride waiting for her wedding night. The grandson told her, "Get up and let your screams tear the heavens to announce the death of Grandfather." And so it was, and the heavens rang with the news.

The grandson opened his eyes. He was still sitting on the mound of the grave among the headstones and cacti. The sun burned the top of his head and his sight was blurred, but little by little he focused on the things around him. The sound of recitation and mourning came to him from afar. He looked at the expanse of the tombs, then trained his gaze on the tomb of al-Qutb, and the ghost of a smile appeared on his face. He looked toward the road leading to the village: the funeral procession was on its way home and had nearly reached the town. The grandson said to himself that he must get up to join the people in offering their condolences.

He picked up his load of books and walked along the road to the village. The closer he got, the louder the recitation grew. Before reaching the village, he turned back to the cemetery and the saint's tomb amid the mass of graves. The grandson approached the village and began to recite. All the men were reciting and all the women were mourning; their voices shook the village to its foundations. The people stood outside the doors of their houses all along both sides of the alley, in rows. The reciters were blind or lame, swollen-bellied or sallow-faced. The children were ill. Men, women, and children. Each person carried death in three-fourths of his body. They recited the Sura of Faith for the soul of the dead man who had been buried: "Say: He is the one God, the Everlasting. He begetteth not, and He was not begotten, and there is none like Him."* The verses were like fluttering banners. The grandson recited, feverish and tearful. He noticed that his voice was very loud and very happy, and very beautiful as well. He laughed, feverish and feeble-minded. He said to himself, in an ecstasy, "We are the ones who carry more death than life in our bodies. Only we know the news of the afterlife. We are the ones who can give life to the mortal world." Then he surrendered his eyes to darkness.

West Berlin
July 1981

*Sura of Faith (Koran 112).